The force of the explosion was huge. The world lit up and there was a deafening roar as the walls of the building blew outwards.

Instinctively, the Delta soldiers had thrown themselves face down on the ground as the explosion hit. Now they stumbled to their feet, taking in the damage.

Mitch began to run towards the building, but Benny grabbed hold of his arm. 'No!' he snapped.

'Gaz is in there!' shouted Mitch.

'If he is, he's dead.'

BOOKS BY JIM ELDRIDGE

BLACK OPS.

DEATH IN THE DESERT

JIM ELDRIDGE

EGMONT

For Lynne, my inspiration as always!

EGMONT

We bring stories to life

Black Ops: Death in the Desert
First published 2010
by Egmont UK Limited
239 Kensington High Street
London W8 6SA

Text copyright © 2010 Jim Eldridge

The moral rights of the author have been asserted

ISBN 978 1 4052 5194 5

3 5 7 9 10 8 6 4 2

www.egmont.co.uk

A CIP catalogue record for this title is available
from the British Library

Typeset by Avon DataSet Ltd, Bidford on Avon, Warwickshire
Printed and bound in Great Britain by the CPI Group

1

As Mitch fell from the plane, the exhilaration of flying hit him. He felt that sudden blast of air ripping at his body as gravity took over.

'When you're jumping at night you have to be visible for three miles in any direction,' his instructor had once told him. That was then. Tonight, his life depended on being invisible. The same went for his comrades.

Mitch brought his legs together and his arms to his sides and rocketed down to the two men who were plummeting towards the Earth below. When he came level with them he opened his arms and legs wide to slow himself, and gripped hands with Gaz on his left and Two Moons on his right to complete the triangular formation. Benny's Texan accent came through the earpiece in his helmet. 'OK, guys. Point of no return. Take it down to 2,000 feet, then separate and open the chutes. We'll keep radio silence from now until you hit the ground. Next contact after the plastic's ready to blow.'

And then there was quiet. The three special-forces soldiers flew downwards through the darkness, riding the air. The sensation of flying was so incredible it was hard to remember they were actually falling at 120 miles per hour.

Below, the outside walls of the castle glowed orange, lit by security lights. Mitch checked the digital display of the altimeter on his wrist, watching the numbers go down. At just the right moment, the men released their grip and moved apart, ready to open their chutes.

Mitch pulled the pilot chute from the bottom of his rig. There was a second's delay while it caught the wind, then it pulled the main chute out. He felt the G-force of deceleration as he slowed to twelve miles per hour. Then he was floating, pulling on the toggles that would steer him directly over the dark surrounds of the castle.

Mitch hit the ground and rolled, hauling his parachute in fast. He heard growling and the thud of running paws: three guard dogs were coming at him, jaws open, their vicious teeth glinting in the moonlight. He pulled out the tranquiliser gun and fired, and the leading dog crumpled to the ground, then lay still. The other dogs also collapsed as Gaz and Two Moons appeared, holstering their own tranquiliser guns. The dogs would be out for about half an hour.

'Right, let's move,' whispered Two Moons.

The three of them made for the castle and then spread out along the front of the building. As he ran, Mitch took the pack from his back and opened it, revealing the explosives inside.

Reaching the castle wall, he worked swiftly, pressing explosives against the stone and at points in the enormous ground-floor windows. When the explosives went off they would take out the supports, leaving the lintel straining under the enormous weight above. If the other guys had fixed their explosives correctly, the stone alcove would come crashing down when they blew. Mitch pushed the detonators into place in the plastic, and then headed for the high outer wall.

Suddenly Mitch sensed a movement to his right. He ducked just in time as a metal bar whistled past his head, glinting in the dim light. Mitch dropped and kicked out at the man, smashing his heel into the side of his assailant's knee. As the man let out a yell of pain, Mitch jumped up and ran for the wall. He could see Two Moons and Gaz already on their way.

Search lights now illuminated the whole area. A voice boomed out from a loud speaker: 'Stop where you are or you will be shot!'

Mitch, Gaz and Two Moons stopped and looked at each other expectantly. From the castle came shouts and the sound of running feet. Armed men were spilling out from the doors.

In Mitch's earpiece, Benny's voice called out, 'What's happening? Situation report!'

Mitch took a deep breath, then said firmly into his mic, 'Plastic's in position! Blow the place up!'

2

Tug looked at Mitch, Two Moons, Gaz and Benny and repeated, 'Blow the place up!' And then he burst out laughing.

'It wasn't funny!' snapped Benny, annoyed.

The five soldiers of Delta Unit, part of the US-UK Combined Special Forces, were in the briefing room at their barracks in London. Troopers Paul Mitchell, Danny Graham and Sergeant Tony Two Moons were telling Captain Robert Tait what a success their practice mission had been, while Lieutenant Bernardo Jaurez was insisting it had been a failure.

'Our mission was to bring the building down,' said Mitch. 'We did it. That building would have collapsed, no problem.'

'But you were supposed to be on the other side of the wall before I set the detonators off!' argued Benny. 'From that distance you would all most likely have been killed.'

'Not necessarily,' Gaz retorted. 'We'd judged the explosives carefully.'

Tug laughed. 'Either way, I wish I'd been there.' He patted his leg. 'The medicos say I'm ready to jump out of a plane again.'

'I'd still go easy,' suggested Mitch. 'It's only been two months since the docs put that leg of yours back together again. When I broke mine a few years ago it was at least four months before I was ready for action.'

'Four months is what they said to me too, at first,' said Tug. 'They offered me a desk job. I told them to forget it. Exercise is what my leg needs, and I'm not going to get it sitting around, pushing paper. So they gave in. I think they got tired of hearing me complain about it.'

Mitch smiled as he looked around at his four

squad mates from Delta Unit. They were a great bunch, he thought. Guys he'd trust with his life.

He, Gaz and Two Moons were the youngest in the unit. Gaz, the short stocky Geordie from Newcastle, was wearing his civvies: jeans and a black leather jacket over a T-shirt with 'Rock 'n' roll' printed on it. With his close-shaven head, tattoos, and Doc Marten boots, he looked more like a roadie for a rock band than a special-forces soldier. Towering above him, Two Moons, the tall Sioux Indian, was loyal and a fierce fighter, frightened of nothing. Today he was dressed almost conservatively, at least by his standards, in a colourful Hawaiian shirt.

Tug, a quiet, softly spoken Englishman, was the son of a lord, but he kept that part of his life separate from his career as a black-ops soldier. Second in command of the unit, under Colonel Chuck Nelson, Tug still limped slightly from the appalling injury he'd suffered on their most recent mission in West Africa. And Benny, a Latino Texan, was the unit's tactician. He'd taken charge of the recent practice and was still upset at the way it had gone.

'The mission was to blow the place up and for you all to get away safely,' he repeated.

'No one said that at the briefing,' said Two Moons, shrugging.

'Because it's so obvious it didn't need saying!'

'Trust me, if it had been a real operation, we'd have got out,' said Mitch confidently. 'We'd have shot the enemy and then got over the wall in the chaos of the explosives going off.'

'You'd have been dead!' insisted Benny.

'No, we wouldn't,' Mitch argued back. 'I'm only dead when I say I'm dead. And even then I'm probably lying.'

'Lying about what?' asked a voice.

They all looked round and saw that Nelson had entered the briefing room. The tall black colonel from Boston was accompanied by another man, Middle Eastern in appearance.

'We were just discussing the recent exercise,' said Tug with a smile. 'There seem to be conflicting opinions on how successful it was.'

Nelson nodded. 'Yes, I heard,' he said. 'Parachuting in at night from high altitude. Good tactic.'

Benny didn't say anything, just sat with a scowl on his face. The games were over, thought Mitch, and it was time to put Benny out of his misery.

'Good tactic, but we messed up, Colonel,' Mitch admitted. 'Only Benny's too good a guy to tell you.'

For a moment Mitch thought Nelson was angry. Mitch was the most recent recruit to Delta Unit, and after his first mission Nelson had threatened to kick him out because of his maverick attitude. Only the support of the other guys had saved his position in the squad. Maybe his 'Blow the place up!' gag had angered his commander.

Instead, to Mitch's relief, Nelson smiled. 'I know exactly what happened,' he said. 'I even got a film of it. Next time, get over the wall before you blow the explosives. Anyway, enough on that. I've got a little treat for you. We're going on a trip.'

'Somewhere warm, I hope?' asked Gaz.

'Somewhere very warm,' Nelson replied, nodding.

'We're going to Afghanistan.'

3

Mitch shot a worried glance at Tug. The captain had seen action in Afghanistan before and it hadn't been a good experience. Behind enemy lines with a four-man unit, Tug had been the only one to come out alive.

Nelson gestured at the man who had come in with him. He was tall and slim, wearing a very smart, expensive-looking suit. This guy is not a soldier, thought Mitch, intrigued. Not if he can afford a suit like that.

'This is Mansur Omari,' said Nelson. Omari smiled in greeting at the soldiers. 'He's the key to this, so I'll let him make his own introductions and he can tell you what the gig is. And then I'll explain how we're gonna do it.' Nelson sat down while Omari moved to a screen at the front of the briefing room.

'Good morning, gentlemen. As the colonel has told you, my name is Mansur Omari and, as you can tell from my accent, I'm an American. I was born and brought up in Chicago. But my family originated from somewhere else, just like pretty much everybody in the States.' Here he smiled and nodded towards Two Moons. 'Except for the Native Americans, such as your colleague, Mr Two Moons.'

Two Moons nodded slightly in acknowledgement. This guy is smooth, thought Mitch. He's got to be a politician of some sort.

Omari continued. 'My parents were originally from Kajaki in Helmand Province in Afghanistan. They left in 1981 during the Soviet invasion to emigrate to America, where I was born a couple of years later. I still have family in Afghanistan, and for the past two years I've been acting as a mediator, working for the United Nations, trying to get peace talks going there.

'The problem is that the official line of both the

US and the UK governments is that they "don't negotiate with terrorists". But, as you know, the war is going badly. Privately both governments accept that they will have to negotiate in some way with the moderate Taliban, who may be willing to talk.'

A PowerPoint display had already been set up. Omari triggered it and a map appeared on the screen: Afghanistan. Mitch was familiar with it, as was every soldier. The area to the south had been highlighted.

So that's where we're going, thought Mitch. Helmand Province. One of the most dangerous places on earth.

'As most of you know, Helmand Province is the hub of insurgent activity,' continued Omari. 'And to make matters worse, it's also the home of the Afghan drugs trade, which provides most of the money to fund the Taliban. And we're not talking small-time drug dealers.'

On the screen appeared a chart showing the structure of the drugs trade in Helmand.

'The Afghans grow poppies from which they extract opium, which is then turned into heroin,' Omari continued. 'In case you didn't know, Colombia produces most of the cocaine that comes into the West, and Morocco most of the cannabis. To put things into perspective, Helmand Province's heroin output provides more street drugs in the West than Colombia and Morocco put together.'

'Why don't we just destroy the poppy fields?' suggested Two Moons. 'No poppies, no opium, no heroin. No money for the Taliban. After all, the Brits have been in Helmand for years. They must know where the poppy fields are.'

'We do,' agreed Tug. 'The troops travel through them when they're on patrol.'

'So why not set fire to them while they're there?' asked Gaz. 'Or, even easier, call in an air attack. A few runs with some napalm would wipe out every poppy field in the place. Several problems solved in one go. No heroin. No Taliban.'

'I'm afraid it's not that simple,' Tug said, sighing.

'We're trying to win the hearts and minds of the Afghan people. Most of the farmers in Helmand Province earn their living by growing poppies for the drugs trade. If we destroyed the poppy fields we'd also destroy their income at the same time. That wouldn't go down well.'

'Persuade them to grow something else,' persisted Two Moons. 'They're farmers. They can grow food. Sell it to Africa. Make money and solve the famine at the same time.' He shook his head and gave a sigh. 'Sure seems simple to me.'

'True,' Omari admitted with a nod, 'but that's without the politics.'

'Ah, the politics!' Two Moons said, chuckling. 'That explains everything!'

The others laughed.

'Back to the matter at hand: the drugs trade and the fighting are carried out by connected groups, led by individual warlords. There are lots of these warlords, each one running his own patch of Helmand, and each with a tough, well-equipped small army. The warlord we're particularly interested in is this one.'

On the screen appeared a picture of a bearded man dressed in loose-fitting robes, his head covered with a black turban. He carried an automatic rifle and had bandoliers of ammunition hanging around his neck and shoulders.

'This is Azma Al Haq, a very powerful Taliban warlord with a stronghold in the mountains in the north of Helmand Province.'

'We gonna kill him?' asked Two Moons.

'I hope not,' said Omari. 'He's my uncle and he's prepared to meet with the UN. We're going to talk to him. Or, rather, I am.'

The soldiers, all except Nelson, looked at one another in surprise.

'Why would he suddenly want to start talking peace?' asked Tug suspiciously.

'I believe he is genuine,' replied Omari. 'I have met my uncle on a few occasions in Afghanistan while working for the UN. He has been fighting all his life. All he's ever wanted is an independent Afghanistan, run by the people. At first the Taliban offered that, but my uncle says that many of the Taliban leaders now are foreigners from Pakistan, not Afghans.

'Over the years some of his children have died in the fighting, as well as his brothers, their wives and daughters. He is an old man now, and he doesn't want his grandchildren and great-grandchildren to go through the same pain and fear of a never-ending war. And the only alternative to war is peace, however difficult that may be to achieve.'

'And you really believe him?' asked Benny.

Omari nodded. 'I do,' he said. 'I met him recently in Kandahar, and made a tentative offer of talks. He agreed – with some conditions.'

'What sort of conditions?' asked Mitch, interrupting.

Omari hesitated, and threw a look at Nelson.

'Need to know basis only, Mitch, I'm afraid,' said Nelson. 'Not our department.'

'It sure would help to know what we were going into,' said Mitch with a shrug.

'I can tell you.' Gaz grinned. 'We're going into trouble.'

The others laughed, and Omari joined in. 'I'm afraid your colleague is right,' he said. 'But a deal with Al Haq could deliver a ceasefire in his part of Helmand. It's been arranged that I will meet him at the only place he really feels safe: his own hideout in the mountains. To get there will mean going through Taliban-controlled territory.'

'And we are going to be Mr Omari's bodyguards,' added Nelson.

'The Taliban will get to hear what's going on,' pointed out Benny. 'Word spreads.'

'Exactly,' agreed Omari. 'So, to stop the extremist Taliban finding out the true nature of our journey, we have concocted a cover story. For which, I'll hand you back to your commander, Colonel Nelson.'

Nelson got up and addressed the unit. 'The reason we gave you the info about the drugs business, the poppy fields and all that, is because our cover story is that we're a bunch of renegade soldiers on our way to do a deal for a very large shipment of heroin from Azma Al Haq.'

'So we're criminals?' asked Two Moons.

'Correct.' Nelson nodded. 'And to make sure the story rings true, it's going to be spread around Pakistan, and other parts of Afghanistan, so that no one knows what's really going on.'

'We could be arrested,' pointed out Tug.

'Worse, we could get killed by rival drug dealers,' said Benny.

'True,' agreed Nelson. 'It's a chance we have to take.'

'And in my opinion, it's worth it,' added Omari. 'If we can put a stop to this conflict we'll save thousands of lives. American, British, Afghan.' He gave a rueful smile. 'I'm American, but I'm also an Afghan. I'm doing this to save people on both sides.'

Nelson looked at the men.

'Well, that's the plan. Any questions?'

'Just one,' said Mitch. To Omari he said, 'If this guy Al Haq is your uncle, why do you need us as your bodyguards?'

'Because my uncle controls the mountain area in the north of Kajaki, but to get there means travelling from Kandahar across forty miles of country controlled by other Taliban warlords, most of them much more hard line than my uncle. And although the Taliban tolerate my uncle because they still see him as an ally, they would do anything to stop him if they thought he was negotiating with the Coalition.'

It was a fair answer, thought Mitch, but something was still nagging him.

'OK, that's it, guys,' said Nelson. 'My next move is to take Mr Omari to the stores and get him kitted out. If he's going to be travelling with us, he's got to look the part.'

'I don't think I'd be any good with weapons,' responded Omari uncertainly.

Nelson grinned at him. 'Don't worry. No weapons, just a uniform.'

With that Nelson and Omari left, and the soldiers got up from their chairs.

'Me, a drug dealer?' Tug said, chuckling. 'Whatever would my father say if he found out?'

Two Moons looked at Mitch and saw the concerned expression on his face. 'You look worried,' he commented.

'Aren't you?' asked Mitch. 'Think about it. This guy we're going in with is a nephew of a Taliban warlord. Doesn't that make you think?'

'About what?'

'About where his loyalties lie?'

'You think Omari is planning to sell us out?' asked Gaz.

'It crossed my mind,' said Mitch.

Gaz laughed. 'You are one paranoid guy, Mitch,' he said. 'The Taliban don't need him to deliver us to them. There are thousands of British and Yank soldiers already there for them to pick up.'

'Yeah, but not a special-forces colonel and his unit.'

Two Moons grinned and slapped Mitch on the shoulder. 'Trust me, this guy Omari's all right,' he said confidently. 'I've got a nose for this kind of thing, and it's kept me alive so far.'

'You were in Afghanistan, Tug,' said Gaz. 'What are the Taliban like as an enemy?'

'Fanatical,' answered Tug, frowning. 'At least, the hard-line ones are. They'll fight to the death.'

4

As their plane circled over Kandahar Airport, Mitch looked out of the window at the landscape below. From the sky it was just a vast expanse of sand, dust and rocks stretching as far as the eye could see, and it was difficult to imagine anyone surviving in this terrain, let alone making a living.

'Military outposts,' pointed out Gaz. Below they could just make out some encampments and vehicles, their colours blending in with the desert.

'It's a hard life out here for those guys,' murmured Tug. 'But trust me, it's even harder behind enemy lines.'

Because they were on a military flight, there were no serious security checks, which meant they were able to bring in their own weapons. Mitch, Gaz and Tug had the British army's standard assault rifle, the SA80. Nelson, Benny and Two Moons preferred the more compact Heckler & Koch G36C.

In addition to their assault rifles, each man carried his preferred close-combat weapons, well hidden. Beneath his uniform, Mitch had a knife strapped to the lower part of each leg, and a H&K Mark 23 pistol inside his combat jacket, within easy reach.

A short time after landing they found themselves inside the airport building.

'You got any contacts here you want to get in touch with?' Nelson asked Omari.

'No,' said Omari. 'Just my uncle in Kajaki.'

'OK, then,' said Nelson. 'Let's go get our vehicles. Time to get this show on the road.'

'One moment, Colonel,' murmured Mitch. 'I think we might have company.'

Benny nodded. 'The guy in the purple suit and

his pals. They started eyeing us when we walked through the gate.'

As casually as they could, the others turned to look.

Nelson grinned.

'Looks like our cover story has worked,' he said. 'Anyone make a guess who they are?'

'I'm guessing they ain't plain-clothes police,' muttered Two Moons.

'And they're not Taliban,' murmured Omari. 'Not in those suits.'

'So, it's the opposition,' Nelson said, nodding. 'OK, I think this is where we send a message to them and anyone else who might be watching us. Who fancies being the bait?'

'Me,' volunteered Mitch. In a louder tone, he said, 'I need to take a leak.' He handed his rifle to Nelson. 'I don't want this getting in the way.'

With that, Mitch headed for the toilet. The men in suits followed. The door to the toilet crashed open behind Mitch and two of the men grabbed him roughly by the arms, while the third jammed the door shut. It was then that Mitch noticed with a shock that there was another door to the toilet, from the outside.

The man in the purple suit produced a pistol, which he pressed to Mitch's head.

'Try and call for help and I'll kill you now,' he threatened.

He ran his hands expertly over Mitch's uniform and found the H&K Mark 23. Finding no other guns strapped to Mitch's thighs, he didn't look further.

The man in the purple suit nodded and the two men holding Mitch pushed him towards the other door. He was forced outside into the bright sun.

'You will walk along with us, without causing a scene,' ordered the man in the purple suit.

'How?' demanded Mitch. 'I've got two guys holding my arms like I'm under arrest.'

The man didn't answer. Instead, he said, 'If you attempt to escape, I will shoot you.'

'Where are we going?' asked Mitch.

The man smiled. 'My boss wishes to talk to you,' he said. 'He's waiting for us in the car park.'

Like hell he is, thought Mitch. They were taking him somewhere quiet to kill him. Then they'd dump his body as a warning to the other 'drug dealers' to stay off their patch. He wondered where Nelson and the other guys were. Surely they would have tried the door to the toilet and found it jammed? They should have busted their way in by now. But it looked like he was going to have to do this on his own. He weighed up the situation and came up with a plan. The question was: when to act?

Mitch looked towards the car park. He'd better make his move here, before they got too far away from the main building. Here, he still had a chance. Once they were in the car park he was as good as dead.

Mitch suddenly stopped and jerked backwards, bringing the two men on each side swinging round in front of him. He headbutted the one on the right and then brought his knee up hard towards the groin of the one on the left. But the man obviously saw it coming, because he blocked Mitch's knee with his thigh and then lashed out, aiming a punch at Mitch's jaw. Mitch jerked back and the man's fist just missed him. Mitch was aware of the man in the purple suit waving the pistol to the right and left, trying to get a clear shot at Mitch.

The man Mitch had headbutted staggered back to his feet and pulled a pistol from inside his jacket. The other man pulled out a handgun.

'Three against one. Naughty naughty!' said a voice behind them.

The men turned, as did Mitch. Nelson, Tug and Gaz stood there, rifles aimed.

'Drop the hardware,' ordered Nelson.

The man in the purple suit glared back at him.

'If you shoot, your own man will die,' he said.

'And so will you,' said Nelson. 'And if we start shooting, these babies have got a lot more firepower than those pop guns you're holding. So drop them.'

The man in the purple suit hesitated, then threw

his pistol on the ground. The other two did the same. Mitch picked up the three guns, and then recovered his own Mark 23.

'You took your time coming,' Mitch complained.

'We wanted to see where they were taking you,' said Nelson.

'Somewhere they could kill me,' said Mitch.

'Yes, that's what we thought.'

'How did you know the toilet had two doors?' asked Mitch.

'I've been here before, remember,' Tug replied. 'Local knowledge always comes in useful.'

Gaz looked at the three men, who were now nervous and fidgety. 'What shall we do with them?' he asked. 'Shoot 'em?'

At this, the three men shuddered and started to back away, but were stopped by Nelson's menacing scowl. 'Not this time,' Nelson said. 'They're not worth it.' He moved right up close to the man in the purple suit, and added in a threatening tone, 'But if we run into you again you won't be so lucky.

Comprende, amigo?'

The man gulped nervously and nodded.

'Good,' Nelson said, smiling. He gestured with his rifle. 'Get!' he snapped.

The three men hesitated, obviously wondering if they would be shot anyway. They began to move away, slowly at first, and then faster, almost breaking into a run.

Nelson, Gaz and Tug relaxed their rifles.

Tug grinned. 'I believe we've just backed up our cover story.'

5

They rejoined Benny, Two Moons and Omari in a military car pound a short walk away from the airport building.

'Everything OK?' asked Two Moons.

Nelson nodded. 'Mitch led them outside and we had a word with them,' he said. 'I don't think they'll come after us again.'

'The main thing is our cover story worked,' said Benny. 'If it stuck with those dealers, hopefully the Taliban believe it too.'

Mitch and the others looked at the three Humvees in front of them. Each vehicle was painted in camouflage colours and bore the scars and marks of hard wear, with dents in the bodywork and chips in the paintwork.

'Tried and tested transport,' announced Nelson proudly.

'They look like wrecks,' commented Two Moons.

'Looks aren't everything,' said Nelson. 'These babies have got armour plating on the body, and underneath. All the windows have bulletproof glass. Four-wheel drive. Six gears. Everything beneath the hood is top notch. There's also a heap of artillery for you in the trunk of the vehicle on your left.'

The soldiers opened the rear of the third Humvee, and lifted the lid off a large metal box. Inside was a bigger selection of weapons than they already carried. More SA80 assault rifles. H&K G36s and 53s. Bushmaster M16s. Daniel Cobray sub-machine guns. Pistols. Knives. A rocket launcher with grenades. A mortar and shells. Semtex explosive. Detonators and timers. It was a whole arsenal. There was also body armour for each of the men.

The boot of the second vehicle contained bundles of clothes. 'Just in case we have to go undercover as locals,' explained Nelson. 'OK, order of travel:

Me and Omari will take the lead because he knows the route. Tug and Benny in the next car. Mitch, Gaz and Two Moons bringing up the rear. OK?'

The men nodded.

'Good. Saddle up and let's go. And keep your eyes peeled. These things have got sensors for picking up and neutralising any roadside bombs, but they won't tell you when a bullet or a rocket is on its way.'

They left the airport in convoy. In the third vehicle Gaz took first turn at the wheel. Mitch sat next to him, with Two Moons in the rear, both with assault rifles resting on their laps, ready to use at the first sign of trouble.

The word 'road' hardly described what they were driving on. It was a surface of sand worn down in parts to rock by the military traffic that had passed over it.

'Just like home,' murmured Two Moons, looking out of the window.

'Come on!' said Mitch, grinning. 'Even Arizona isn't this bare.'

'Delta One to convoy. Everyone OK back there?' came Nelson's voice over their radio.

'Delta Two fine,' came Tug's voice.

Gaz pressed the com switch. 'Delta Three fine,' he said.

They rumbled on.

'Either of you guys know much about this Kajaki place we're going to?' asked Two Moons.

'I've got a friend, Jimmy, who did a tour of duty here with the Northumbrians six months ago,' said Gaz. 'According to Jimmy, Kajaki is very much Taliban territory.'

'Then I guess the chance that we'll run into either Taliban or Coalition forces on the way is pretty high,' said Mitch.

Two Moons grunted sourly. 'At the speed this heap is going we'll be lucky to run into anything,' he said. 'Even a tortoise could get out of our way in time.'

The three Humvees continued across the desert and then began a slow climb as the road moved to higher ground, twisting and turning around low mountains. There had been no sign of any other people. No villages or houses, just bare desert.

They kept their distance from Tug and Benny's vehicle, but even then the dust from the car in front swirled around them. They had just slowed down to take a bend in the road when Mitch felt the ground beneath the car begin to shake and heard a loud rumbling. Through the dust Mitch saw a huge boulder bounce down the steep slope to their right, making straight for them.

6

'Look out!' yelled Mitch.

'Got it!' Gaz shouted back. He was already ramming his foot on the accelerator to try to speed past the boulder, but it was no good. The boulder smashed into the side of the Humvee, sending it careering off the road and down a steep slope. For a second they looked to be in danger of rolling over, but Gaz managed to steer the vehicle into a slide, churning up huge clouds of dust as he did so.

Mitch had already switched on the com and shouted: 'Delta Three. Possible ambush!'

Gaz slammed his foot on the brakes, but the momentum of the heavy vehicle was against them as they hurtled towards the next ridge, which dropped away down the side of the mountain.

'Abandon ship!' yelled Gaz.

All three kicked open their doors. Out of the corner of his eye, Mitch saw Two Moons hurl himself out, and Gaz getting ready to jump, then he launched himself from the armoured car, still keeping a firm grip on his automatic rifle. He hit the ground with a jarring thud and rolled to take the force of the landing, sliding on sand and pebbles before coming up against hard rock.

The vehicle slid down the slope and disappeared over the edge in a cloud of dust.

Mitch pushed himself up on to his knees, rifle cradled in his arms ready to fire, eyes alert, searching for any movement that would give the enemy away. Two Moons was also now up, rifle poised for action. He swung from side to side and bobbed up and down as he moved, to stop any sniper getting a clear aim at him.

Where was Gaz? Mitch couldn't see him, but the air was still thick with dust and sand. Mitch stood up and headed for the ridge below him, scanning the area in case Gaz was lying injured.

Two Moons joined him and they looked down. Their vehicle was lying on its side about three hundred feet below, on another section of the mountain track. 'Any sign of Gaz?' asked Two Moons urgently.

Mitch shook his head. 'Stay here and watch my back,' he said. 'I'm going down to the vehicle.'

As he slid over the ridge and began to climb down the steep slope of sand and pebbles, he heard Nelson's voice bark in his headset: 'Situation report?'

'Two Moons and I are OK,' said Mitch. 'We got out before the vehicle went over the ridge. It's at the bottom of the next slope down. No sign of Gaz. I thought he jumped out too, but maybe he got trapped. I'm going down to see.'

'Be careful!' said Nelson. 'Benny and I are coming to you. Tug's staying with Omari.'

Mitch continued down the slope, eyes and ears alert, but there was no sign or sound of an enemy.

He reached the vehicle, which was lying on its passenger side. The driver's door was hanging open. Mitch climbed up and looked inside. Gaz wasn't there.

He checked the ground around the vehicle. There were marks which led along the track and then disappeared into a cluster of rocks.

A sound behind Mitch made him whirl round. It was Nelson. He gestured at the vehicle and asked, 'Gaz?'

Mitch shook his head. 'There's no sign of him.'

'Maybe he managed to get out and is lying somewhere nearby,' suggested Nelson.

Again, Mitch shook his head. He pointed to the scuff marks and tracks. 'There are signs of at least three people here. My guess is that Gaz has been taken prisoner.'

Nelson frowned. 'That quickly?'

'They must have had people lying in wait all around here,' said Mitch. 'Then the ones nearest Gaz pounced on him, and the rest skedaddled.'

In their headsets they heard Benny's voice. 'The area here seems secure. No hostiles in sight. What's the situation down there?'

'Gaz is gone,' replied Nelson. 'Looks like he's been taken prisoner.' He swore, then looked ruefully at the vehicle. 'I think we're going to need some help to push this thing back on its wheels.'

7

Working together, they managed to push the Humvee upright. Then they towed it back on to the main road using the two other vehicles. Mitch's mind was racing. Where was Gaz? He couldn't have been taken far – there hadn't been much time. But then it only took a few seconds to kidnap someone, and their attackers would know the area inside out.

Nelson stood surveying the surrounding country-side through binoculars. He could see a small village not too far away. Maybe Gaz had been taken there.

'OK, Mr Omari,' said Nelson. 'Who d'you reckon did this? Taliban? Al-Qaeda?'

'No,' replied Omari, shaking his head.

'How can you be so sure?' asked Mitch.

'Look at the weapon they used,' said Omari.

'A big boulder rolled down the slope. It's out of the Stone Age. And they didn't shoot at any of us. That doesn't mean they don't have weapons, it just means they didn't want to get caught up in a fire-fight with you. If they'd been top military Taliban they'd have carried on with the ambush. The fact that they disappeared as soon as they'd got your man makes me think that was the whole point of it. Snatch a prisoner and then get away safely.'

'Makes sense,' murmured Nelson.

'So you don't think Gaz is dead?' asked Mitch.

Omari shook his head. 'If he had been, they'd have left his body here. It seems to me they wanted a live prisoner. Which means a hostage. A bargaining chip.'

'Show him on TV and threaten to cut off his head unless the infidel Yanks and Brits get out of Afghanistan?' mused Nelson.

Omari nodded.

'So now I suppose we wait for a message, offering

him back in return for a ransom?' asked Tug.

'I don't think so,' replied Omari. 'The people who did this are just locals. My guess is they were acting on instructions from someone more important. I'm pretty sure the same message will have gone out to everybody in the area. This lot just struck lucky.'

'So how do we find out who's holding Gaz?' asked Mitch.

Omari gestured at the nearby village. 'Local information,' he said. 'But I'm afraid they're only likely to give that to another local. Or, at least, another Afghan. If you go in wearing those uniforms you'll get nothing.'

'Then we dress up in the local outfits we got,' said Nelson.

'Forgive me, Colonel, but you'd never pass for an Afghan,' said Omari.

'You ain't goin' alone,' said Nelson. 'Our mission is to get you to Kajaki.'

'I'll go with him,' said Tug. 'I speak some Pushtu, so I'll be able to understand what's going on.'

'And me,' said Two Moons.

'Me, too,' added Mitch.

Nelson nodded. 'OK,' he said. 'Me and Benny will wait here. But take care. I don't want to lose the rest of you as well.'

Mitch, Two Moons, Tug and Omari changed into local costume from the selection in the car, putting on the robes and scarves over their body armour. 'Won't they think it's strange us turning up in one of these things?' asked Two Moons, gesturing at the Humvee.

'No, there are many of these vehicles in use in this country,' said Omari. 'Some of them captured from the Western armies.'

They jumped into the car and set off, with Two Moons at the wheel.

'How are you going to get the info we need?' Mitch asked Omari. 'These sorts of things usually take time.'

'And time is one thing we don't have,' added Tug. 'The longer Gaz is a prisoner, the harder it's going to be to find him and get him back.'

Omari patted a pocket in his robe. 'I have money,' he said. 'And the people here are very poor.'

'You're going to bribe them?' asked Two Moons. 'That doesn't always work. Trust me, the tribe I come from are poor and if someone offered them money to give up one of their own, they'd chase them off.'

'True,' agreed Omari. 'But *someone* will take the money. It's a question of finding out who.'

'And how will you know that?' asked Tug.

Omari shrugged. 'I will know,' he said. 'A gesture here, a look there. The little signs.' As the vehicle neared the cluster of buildings, Omari said, 'This is a small village. It might be advisable if only one of you came out of the vehicle with me. We are here to ask for help, not to intimidate these people.'

'That's your opinion,' growled Mitch. 'If it gets Gaz back, I'm prepared to intimidate anyone.'

'Easy, Mitch,' said Tug. 'What Omari says makes sense. Trust me, I've been here before. I suggest you go with Omari while Two Moons and I wait in the car.'

'Why me?' asked Mitch.

'Because if anyone comes up to the car to find out what we're up to, I can talk to them in Pushtu. And you pass as Afghan better than Two Moons does.'

'Makes sense,' agreed Mitch. The vehicle pulled to a halt close to the nearest small clay building.

'OK,' said Tug. 'Go find out where Gaz is.'

'I assume it's not a problem if I take my gun,' said Mitch, gesturing at his weapon.

Omari smiled. 'Out here, men feel undressed if they aren't carrying an automatic rifle,' he said.

'Keep in view,' said Tug. 'If things go bad, we'll cover you.'

8

Omari headed straight for the nearest house in the village. He seemed confident. This struck Mitch as suspicious. Omari had told them that this area was controlled by hard-line warlords, so why didn't he seem worried being here?

When they reached the house there was much talking, smiling, and – Mitch noticed – money changing hands discreetly. At one point the man Omari was talking to scowled, darted a glance further into the village, and spat on the ground, at which Omari nodded sympathetically. Mitch hadn't a clue what was being said, and part of him wished Tug had come. With his knowledge of Pushtu he would be able to tell Mitch what was really going on. Without Tug, Mitch just had to trust Omari.

And right now, he was wary about doing that.

The conversation must have yielded some kind of result, because Omari turned and headed towards another house further into the village. Mitch grabbed Omari's arm and stopped him. 'Wait,' he warned. 'Where are we going?'

'I have the name of a man in the village who may be able to help us,' Omari told him. 'I am told he is a cheat and a liar and will do anything for money. He is not to be trusted. Which means he knows everything that goes on in this area.' Omari indicated a narrow alleyway. 'He lives down there.'

'But if we go there we'll be out of sight of Tug and Two Moons,' said Mitch.

'True,' Omari admitted. 'But I do not think this man is dangerous.'

'But he may have friends who are,' persisted Mitch.

Omari smiled. 'Then I hope you are quick with that rifle,' he said.

With that, he moved down the narrow alleyway.

Mitch swore under his breath. If this is a trap and I get captured as well, Nelson is going to kill me! he thought.

Omari was heading towards a shabby hut made of clay and mud. He rapped at the wooden door, and when it opened he launched into a rapid burst of Pushtu, smiling winningly all the while. The bearded man at the door looked out at Omari suspiciously, his expression becoming even more mistrustful when he saw Mitch. But Omari produced a bundle of notes from his robe. That did the trick. The man stepped aside from the door and ushered them in.

Inside, with the windows shuttered, the room was dark. The conversation between Omari and the bearded man became more serious. The smiles vanished. Mitch picked up words like 'Yankee' and 'British' in between the bearded man's Pushtu. Omari listened, nodding, and asked more questions, all the time holding the bundle of notes. Mitch noticed the bearded man's gaze kept flicking towards the money.

Mitch was tense, his ears alert for intruders creeping up on the house. He felt isolated here, with just his rifle to protect them. He shouldn't have come down the alleyway without letting Two Moons and Tug know, but Omari had moved so swiftly and determinedly. And they were trying to find Gaz, so there was no time to spare.

Finally Omari peeled off several notes from the bundle and handed them to the man. Omari was smiling again. The two men bowed to one another, and then Mitch followed Omari back out into the sunshine.

'What did he say?' asked Mitch, as the door shut behind them.

'I'll tell you later,' said Omari. 'We have to move fast if we are to save your friend.'

Omari hurried back down the narrow alleyway, Mitch hot on his heels. They got back to the vehicle and found Tug standing outside it, an angry expression on his face.

'I told you to keep in sight!' he said.

'Tell him that,' said Mitch, gesturing at Omari.

'I think I know where your friend might be,' said Omari.

'*Might* be?' asked Tug.

'It's the best I could do in a short time,' said Omari. 'But I'm pretty sure the information I have is correct.'

'What makes you so sure?' asked Tug.

'Because the man knew that if he lied to me, you would go back and kill him.'

Omari didn't reveal the information he'd got until they had rejoined Nelson and Benny, who were waiting by the other two vehicles. As they got out, Nelson hurried towards them. 'What have you got?' he demanded impatiently.

'If my information is correct, I believe your man is being held by a gang of youths led by a young extremist who came out here from England. His mother is English but his father is Pakistani. He calls himself Ajaz al Muhadeen. He has come out here to take part in what he calls the Holy War,' Omari explained.

'Because of his parents?' asked Nelson.

Omari shook his head. 'Apparently not. It seems this young man was radicalised by fundamentalists in Britain. His father and mother are ashamed of him and have disowned him.'

'And where is this Ajaz al Muhadeen?' asked Benny.

'In the next village,' said Omari. 'The people around here aren't happy that he's come because he's stirring things up with their sons. Radicalising them. Unfortunately, there are a handful of boys with nothing to do, and he's formed a gang. They've got guns.' He sighed. 'Ajaz al Muhadeen seems determined to make a name for himself so he will be welcomed by the Taliban as some kind of hero. If what that man said is true, taking your friend is the first part of that.'

'It's also the last part!' snapped Nelson. 'Where is this village?'

9

Nelson and Tug lay on the rocks and used binoculars to scan the village that lay two miles away down on the flat plain. Mitch, Two Moons and Benny were with Omari, standing beside the three vehicles, hidden out of sight in a rock gulley.

Nelson and Tug joined the others.

'What's the score?' asked Benny.

'It's a small village just like any other,' said Nelson. 'Once we're down from these hills there's no cover between us and it. Just open country. Scrub and desert. If we go in with our Humvees we could alarm them. If what we've been told is true, the guys holding Gaz are just kids – they'll be nervous and trigger happy. If they start shooting, Gaz is going to be the first one to get it.'

'So we crawl over there, keeping low,' suggested Two Moons. 'Two miles on our knees is nothing. We do it all the time.'

'My worry is we'll get spotted,' mused Benny. 'It just needs one guy out herding his goats or whatever to see a slight movement and we'll be sitting ducks. I know what it's like for the people out here. My grandparents were Mexican sheep farmers. They sat around most of the day looking out at the land, watching for lizards and stuff. If anything moved they'd notice it and talk about it for days, even if it was just a jack rabbit.'

'OK,' said Nelson. 'So how about this? No crawling, no covert stuff. We just walk straight in.'

'Dressed as locals?' asked Mitch.

Nelson nodded. 'Four of us go in. One of us needs to stay here and watch Omari.'

'I'll be fine,' insisted Omari.

'If you were going to be fine, you wouldn't have needed us in the first place,' argued Nelson. 'Benny, you stay here with Omari.'

Benny shook his head.

'Colonel, I hate to be insubordinate, but don't you think the sight of a black man in a robe might trigger a few suspicions?'

'I could be Somali,' said Nelson. 'There's loads of Islamic fundamentalists from Africa here.'

The others looked at him doubtfully.

Nelson sighed and shrugged. 'OK,' he said. 'I'll stay here and look after Omari. You guys go get Gaz.'

Gaz flexed his wrists and ankles against the ropes that held him to the chair, but the knots had been well tied. There was no way he was going to get free of them.

He looked around. He was in a single-storey house made of mud and brick, but the room had been turned into a small makeshift TV studio. A video camera on a tripod stood with its lens and microphone facing him, although at the moment both were switched off. He guessed the village only got electricity for a short time each day.

He looked at the two young men – probably aged fifteen or sixteen – who had been left to guard him. They sat cross-legged on the floor, talking in the local dialect. Both of them had automatic rifles lying across their laps. Ammunition was stacked in boxes around the room.

This place is a real ammo dump, Gaz thought. The house they'd first thrown him into had been piled high with home-made bombs, detonators lying around casually. He had smelt the fertiliser used to make the explosives. These kids meant business.

He wondered where they intended to use the bombs. Roadsides? To attack Coalition positions? Or maybe they were for suicide bombers? Pack a load of that stuff into a car and ram it into a building and *Boom!* Goodbye to the bomber and everyone for half a mile around.

He heard footsteps approaching from outside, and the two kids got to their feet, standing ready with their rifles aimed at the door. It opened and the leader of the group entered. Ajaz al Muhadeen. Like the others, he carried an automatic rifle.

He stomped over to Gaz and stood in front of him. 'The electricity comes back on in an hour,' he said. 'Are you ready to say what needs to be said for the camera?'

'If it needs to be said, you say it,' replied Gaz. 'No one's going to watch it anyway. Except your mates back home.' Gaz grinned. 'That's what all this is about, isn't it? Impressing your mates. Showing them the stupid little runt they used to make fun of reckons he's a Big Man in Afghanistan.'

Al Muhadeen scowled and punched Gaz high on the forehead. For a second it looked as if the soldier was going to tip over backwards, but he managed to steady the chair.

Gaz grinned once again at Al Muhadeen. 'That'll look good on camera,' he said mockingly. 'A man with bruises all over his face. Still going to say I spoke of my own free will?'

Al Muhadeen looked as if he was about to punch

Gaz again, but he stopped himself. Instead, he bent down and pushed his face right up against Gaz's. 'You are the enemy!' he spat. 'You come here and defile my country . . . '

'This isn't your country,' Gaz reminded him. 'I've heard you talking on your mobile to your pals back home in England.'

'England isn't my home!' Al Muhadeen burst out.

'What about your parents?' said Gaz.

'My parents are no longer true to the faith!' ranted Al Muhadeen. 'I am freeing my people from the invaders!' He rammed the barrel of his rifle into Gaz's chest. 'You will talk to the camera!' he ordered. 'You will say that you and your kind are wrong. You will call on the governments of Britain and America to remove all their troops from this country.'

Gaz smiled. 'Yes, they'll take notice of that,' he said mockingly. 'I can just hear the president of the US of A saying, "There's a fella there from Newcastle gonna get his head cut off unless I withdraw our troops and let Osama bin Laden plot against my country."' Gaz laughed. 'In your dreams, pal!'

Al Muhadeen's expression tightened. 'You have less than an hour. When the electricity comes back, you will talk – or your death will be shown around the world.'

'Will my family get royalties?' asked Gaz.

Al Muhadeen gritted his teeth. 'Trust me, you won't find being killed so funny,' he hissed.

The four men of Delta Unit tramped in single file along the dusty track towards the village. Really, it wasn't even a village, just a cluster of single-storey mud and brick buildings.

'If this is a trap we'll be picked off one by one,' grunted Two Moons. 'We should have gone for the stealth option.'

'If it is a trap, we'd be caught either way,' Mitch said in a low voice.

As they drew nearer to the small settlement they

caught sight of movement in some of the houses. People were watching them through the windows. Then the door of the nearest house opened, and a man stepped out. Like them, he carried an automatic rifle.

'No shooting until we get right up close,' ordered Tug. 'Unless they start shooting first.'

The man who had come out of the house stood in the doorway, waiting for them. His rifle remained pointed down at the ground, but each soldier kept his eyes on him, ready to take action if he made a move.

The man was dressed in local traditional dress, a long shirt over loose cotton trousers, but his head was bare. As they drew near the house, the man called out a greeting. Tug responded curtly in Pushtu.

'What did he say?' whispered Benny.

'Just giving us his greetings,' said Tug.

They were all tense, fingers hovering over triggers and ready to fire. Just a few more yards would put them close enough to throw stun grenades in through the doorway and a window, disabling the enemy.

They drew nearer, and now they could see the man at the door clearly. He seemed very young, his attempt at a beard was straggly and thin. Again, he called out to them, but this time something in his voice had changed, and the soldiers hesitated.

And then the house blew up.

10

The force of the explosion was huge. The world seemed to light up and there was a deafening roar as the walls blew outwards. The young man standing by the door was engulfed in flames. He screamed and then collapsed, disappearing from sight in a thick cloud of black smoke.

Instinctively, the Delta soldiers had thrown themselves face down on the ground as the explosion hit. Now they stumbled to their feet, taking in the damage to the house. With its walls blown out, the roof had collapsed and they could see the burning shell through the smoke.

Mitch began to run towards the building, but Benny grabbed hold of him. 'No!' he snapped.

'Gaz is in there!' shouted Mitch.

'If he is, he's dead,' said Benny curtly.

People from the other houses in the village were running towards the explosion, screaming and yelling in panic. Mitch noticed more young men appearing from one of the buildings, wearing the same long straggly beards and carrying automatic rifles.

'There!' he said, pointing urgently.

Mitch headed for the house at a run, Two Moons and Benny following him, while Tug dropped to a crouch, ready to lay down covering fire at the first sign of trouble.

The door of the second house was ajar, and Mitch threw himself through it.

Gaz was sitting tied to a chair, bound with thick ropes. A relieved grin crossed his face at the sight of his team.

Mitch set to work freeing Gaz, while Two Moons and Benny guarded the door. 'Anyone else here?' he asked.

'No, they've all legged it. What was that? An air attack?'

'I think someone accidentally blew themselves up,' said Two Moons.

There was a burst of gunfire from outside, and Benny shouted, 'We've got company!'

'I'll take it!' yelled Two Moons, and he ran off with Benny while Mitch released the last of the ropes that bound Gaz to the chair.

When Gaz was free, the two ran outside. A gun battle was in progress, with Benny and Two Moons firing from the cover of the house, and Tug in a position near the burning wreckage of the explosion.

Mitch let off a burst with his own gun. One of the young men dropped his rifle and crumpled to the ground. Others lay near the wrecked building. There were now only two men left standing.

'That's Al Muhadeen,' Gaz shouted above the noise of the gunfire, pointing at one of the pair.

Tug called out something in Pushtu. Mitch didn't understand the words, but he got the impression Tug was giving them a chance to surrender. Instead, both of them fired at Tug, who dived for cover behind a nearby rock. As bullets bounced and ricocheted all around him, the rest of Delta Unit directed a hail of bullets at the two men. When Benny saw Gaz with Mitch he shouted out, 'Time to go!'

The soldiers headed for the track that would take them out of the village. Mitch, Tug and Two Moons ran backwards at speed, keeping their guns trained on the village in case of a surprise attack, while Benny hurried Gaz along. They weren't followed and the only sounds coming from the village were wails and screams of distress and the crackling of the burning building.

11

The convoy was on the move again, across flat sandy tracks: Nelson and Omari in the first vehicle; Benny and Tug in the second; and Two Moons at the wheel of the third, with Gaz and Mitch. This was the first time Mitch and Two Moons had had a chance to talk properly to Gaz since the rescue. Nelson had decided to put as much distance as possible between them and the village as fast as they could.

'What happened to you, Gaz?' Mitch asked. 'I thought you jumped out of the vehicle when we did. I saw you!'

'I did,' admitted Gaz sheepishly. 'But the strap of my rifle got caught on the steering wheel. By the time I'd managed to free myself it was too late: the vehicle had gone over the edge and was rolling over and over. I thought I was a gonner, going over a mountain in that thing.' He rubbed the side of his head. 'I must have hit my head and sort of knocked myself out. Anyway, the thing stopped rolling and I was groggy. Next thing, I'm being dragged out and over the rocks. Bang! Someone hit me on the head and that was it. Lights out.' He shrugged. 'After that, it was just a case of waiting for the chance to get away. Or for you lot to come and rescue me.'

Two Moons shook his head. 'I still can't get over that building blowing up like that. If we'd been any closer it would have been lights out for the lot of us.'

'Why did it blow up?' asked Mitch.

'That was their ammo store,' said Gaz. 'Bullets, and loads of home-made explosives. It's where they dumped me when they first got me to the village. My guess is they were planning to carry out some kind of bombing campaign. Or maybe they were just making improvised explosive devices there. I bet one of those idiots dropped a cigarette end or something, a bit too close to the IEDs.'

'Who were they?' asked Two Moons. 'Omari says that their leader was from the UK.'

Gaz gave a wry laugh. 'Leader?' he scoffed. 'He was a lunatic who thought he was a cross between Che Guevara and Robin Hood. He'd gathered this group of young guys from the nearby villages, convinced them that they had to strike a blow for freedom. Amateurs!'

'He may have been an amateur but they got you away pretty neatly,' Mitch pointed out.

'True,' Gaz admitted. 'He'd had training, you could see that. But he had no real strategy.'

'What did they want you for?' asked Two Moons.

'You saw the set-up in the room?' asked Gaz.

Two Moons shook his head. 'No, I was too busy dealing with the bad guys.'

'I did,' said Mitch. 'Camera. Lights. Just your average home-movie kit.'

'They had a generator which gave them electricity for an hour or so a day,' said Gaz. 'They wanted to film me appealing for the Brits and Yanks to leave

69

the country. They also wanted me to apologise for all the wrongs we've done.'

'So how much footage did they get?'

'Not much,' said Gaz. 'I refused to give them the answers they wanted. So they beat me up a little. And threatened to do terrible things to me if I didn't comply. That was all they really got on camera: me getting beaten up.' He sighed. 'Pity I didn't get my hands on the tape. Someone might still post it on YouTube.'

Mitch smiled as he reached into his pocket and produced a video cassette. 'No, they won't,' he said. 'I took it out of the camera just before we left.'

'Well done, pal!' said Gaz, chuckling. 'At least I'll have a memento of this mission!'

12

The convoy continued on its journey. Mitch was now at the wheel of the third vehicle, with Two Moons in the passenger seat and Gaz in the back. They were more alert than ever for sudden attacks, from rocks and boulders, or from more modern weapons. Travelling over this sandy terrain was slow.

'I sure would hate to be doing this as a sightseeing trip,' grunted Two Moons. 'Twenty miles an hour, and the same scenery the whole way. Sand and rocks.'

'The beauty of the desert,' said Mitch. 'That's what everyone says.'

'Those people don't have to sit in a tin can bumping along at this speed,' Two Moons complained. 'If you can call the pace we're going at "speed".'

'Maybe we should have used camels,' said Gaz.

'They travel over this sort of country easy.'

'You ever ridden a camel?' asked Mitch.

'Yep,' replied Gaz. 'In Morocco.' He grinned. 'The thing spat in my face and wouldn't get up when I wanted to go, or slow down when I wanted to stop. Stupid creatures. Give me a tin can like this any time.'

Ahead of them they could see a village, much larger than the previous one. Mitch estimated there were about a hundred houses, all of them single storey. They could see that the other two vehicles had already pulled up in what looked like a village square, and the men had got out. Mitch eased the vehicle alongside the others, and they joined the rest of Delta Unit.

'What's going on, Colonel?' asked Two Moons.

'Pit stop,' said Nelson. 'Omari says he knows these people and it will be a safe place for a break. He suggests we make it an overnight stay rather than camping out in the desert.'

They looked around them. The villagers had

stayed indoors, but the men were all aware that they were being watched from the houses.

'D'you reckon our cover story's reached this place?' asked Benny.

'This is Afghanistan,' said Omari. 'Word spreads. I'm pretty sure they'll know why we're here.'

'And they don't mind drug dealers?' asked Mitch.

Omari shrugged. 'It's business.' Turning to Nelson, he added, 'It's customary to greet the headman of the village and introduce ourselves.'

'Lead the way,' said Nelson.

They followed Omari to a house at one corner of the square. As they walked, Mitch kept a firm grip on his rifle and his eyes scanned the surrounding houses. He noticed that the rest of the men did the same.

'Great building material, mud,' commented Tug. 'Keeps the house warm in winter, cool in summer. And bullets don't go through it as easily as they do wood and steel.'

'It still blows up,' grunted Mitch, remembering

what had happened in the last village.

A tall man had come out of the house they were heading for. He was accompanied by other senior villagers, while several women watched the soldiers from just inside the house itself.

'This is Parwaz Shah, the malik, or village headman,' said Omari, doing the introductions.

As the rest of Delta Unit nodded, Tug greeted him in Pushtu.

'I'm impressed,' said Omari. 'You speak Pushtu well.'

'I was in the mountains in Afghanistan before,' said Tug.

'Searching for Osama bin Laden?'

'Well, I wasn't on a camping holiday,' Tug replied with a grin.

Omari spoke to Parwaz Shah, gesturing at the men of Delta Unit and their vehicles, and Shah nodded.

'What's he saying?' Mitch asked Tug.

'He's telling them that we're here on business,

74

and that we're on our way to meet a man in the mountains to the north.'

'And that's it?' asked Mitch.

Omari nodded. 'That's enough for them to work out what they think is really going on. Anything less would be impolite, especially if we're going to receive hospitality from them.'

Now the introductions had been made, other villagers came forward, keen to look at the new arrivals. The children especially were bursting with curiosity. The Delta Unit soldiers smiled at the villagers.

'Looks like the whole village has turned out to check us over,' said Mitch.

The children mostly smiled back at them, although a few looked at them suspiciously and hid behind their parents. The men wore traditional clothing. The children were all barefoot, and wore very little in the way of clothes. The women were mostly dressed in long shirts which hung down over their full-length skirts. All of them wore a shawl tied loosely around their heads.

'I thought the women all wore the burqa?' said Gaz. None were wearing the outfit that covers Muslim women from head to foot.

'You'll find that in the towns and bigger villages,' explained Omari. 'Here, the large shawl they wear draped over their heads – the hijab – is deemed sufficient. Unless they're in an area under strict Taliban rule.'

Two Moons had been looking out over the fields that extended from one side of the village.

'What are they growing there?' he asked. 'It sure don't look like poppies.'

'It's not,' said Tug. 'It's wheat and rice.'

'How come the war hasn't touched this place?' asked Nelson.

'Oh, it's touched them, all right,' said Omari. 'Two years ago they were accidentally bombed by Coalition planes. Someone gave out the wrong coordinates or something. Six villagers were killed, including four children.'

'So maybe they're looking for revenge while we're here?' murmured Mitch.

'They've also had visits from the Taliban, who felt that they weren't religious enough,' said Omari. 'The bodies of villagers from those visits are buried outside. Trust me, these people are no fans of the Taliban, either. Right now all they want to do is get on with their lives. But they will give us hospitality. Food, and a roof over our heads for the night. It's the custom here.' He smiled. 'Of course, some kind of return gesture would be greatly appreciated. This is a very poor village. They've got a generator, but it only provides electricity very briefly each day. There's no school here, so there are no books.'

'So cash would be appreciated?' asked Nelson.

Omari nodded. 'Cash is always appreciated,' he said. He patted the pocket of his robe. 'I'll deal with it.'

Two Moons leaned in to Mitch and muttered, 'That guy's walking around with a robe stuffed full of money. I wouldn't feel safe doin' that in the US, let alone here.'

Mitch shrugged. 'So far he's got Gaz back for us, and we're all still alive,' he said. 'I guess we have to trust he knows what he's doing.'

13

The evening air was warm. Delta Unit sat outside, cross-legged on the ground, eating the meal the villagers had prepared for them. The food was excellent: fresh vegetables with rice, soup with flat nan bread, followed by yoghurt, and rounded off with almonds covered in sugar.

Mitch noticed that Tug seemed agitated. He was constantly glancing around and he was obviously listening out for any unusual sounds.

'Something make you uneasy about this, Tug?' asked Mitch.

'Just being in this country makes me uneasy,' admitted the captain. He gestured at the village. 'This is exactly the sort of village we were in when I was here before. A situation similar to this: behind

79

enemy lines on a covert mission. And we were treated with hospitality and friendship just like we are being shown now.' He grimaced bitterly. 'And then they sold us out to the Taliban.' He gave a deep sigh at the memory. 'I was the only one of our unit who got out alive.'

'So you don't trust them?'

Tug shook his head. 'No,' he said. 'The headman here seems fine, but so did the last one. We never knew who ratted us out. It may have been him, it may not. It could have been someone else in the village who just didn't like us. Or maybe someone in the village was Taliban. All I know is the Taliban came in and hit us. I was lucky there was a US helicopter patrol in the area around the same time. They got me out.'

After they'd eaten, Nelson allocated the watch rota: Mitch and Two Moons, followed by Nelson and Benny, and finally Tug and Gaz. Mitch was glad to take first watch. He always had difficulty getting to sleep and with a later watch he would often fall asleep only minutes before he was due to wake up and go on duty.

'I reckon the best place will be on one of those flat roofs,' suggested Two Moons. 'One of the houses near the vehicles. That way we'll have a view over the desert and we can keep an eye on our transport.'

'I was thinking the same,' agreed Mitch.

Through Omari, they asked permission to go up on the roof, then climbed up to the vantage point. The rest of the unit, along with Omari, disappeared into the houses around the square where beds had been prepared for them.

Mitch and Two Moons sat just behind the low wall at the edge of the roof, rifles cradled in their laps.

'Peaceful,' commented Two Moons, looking out over the desert.

'Only for the moment,' said Mitch. 'The calm before the storm.'

'You think we're going to pull this off? You think

we're going to get Omari to meet his uncle?'

'Yes, I do.' Mitch nodded. Then he added ruefully, 'But whether we make it out again safely afterwards, that's another matter.'

Mitch felt himself being shaken awake.

'Wake up! We've got company!'

The urgency in Two Moons' voice jolted Mitch wide awake as if he'd been doused with icy cold water. He always slept with his rifle beside him, and it was in his hands even before he had swung his feet off the wooden bed. Light was coming through the window.

'Who's coming?' he demanded.

'Taliban,' said Two Moons. 'Tug and Gaz spotted them. Gaz is still on the roof.'

'They in vehicles?'

Two Moons shook his head. 'On foot.'

'Let's go,' said Mitch.

Two Moons hurried off and Mitch hastily pulled on his boots, then rushed after him. Outside in the square, Parwaz Shah, Nelson, Benny, Tug and Omari were talking urgently.

Mitch ran to the Humvee where Two Moons was already unloading a rocket-propelled grenade launcher, a mortar, and the grenades and shells for them.

'We may not need these,' Two Moons said, 'but I'd rather have them ready than go out looking for them when the shooting starts.'

The two men hauled the artillery up on to one of the flat roofs overlooking the desert where the Taliban fighters had appeared. Keeping down so they wouldn't be spotted, they dragged the weapons across to the low wall. Mitch took a quick look out into the desert. He could see the approaching group of Taliban fighters. There were about fifteen men, walking in single file. All of them wore a mixture of black and white: the traditional baggy cotton trousers, flowing shirts and waistcoats, black turbans wrapped round their heads.

Within two minutes everything was primed and ready.

'OK, I'm set up,' said Two Moons. 'You'd better get below and see what's happening.'

Mitch went back down the brick steps to the square, where Omari was still engaged in a hurried and intense conversation with Shah. It was obvious that Shah was very frightened.

Omari turned to the soldiers. 'He says the Taliban are coming here because they think this village is backsliding. They're coming to teach them a lesson and bring them into line.'

'Which means?'

'Killing those who offend them most,' said Omari. 'That's what they did last time they came.'

Nelson shook his head. 'That ain't happening on my watch.' He looked at the rest of the unit. 'You guys OK with that?'

'Do you have to ask?' retorted Mitch. He was already checking his rifle for ammo.

'We can't risk a gun battle inside the village,'

said Tug. 'There are too many civilians.'

'We'll put up a defensive line,' Nelson told them. 'We'll use the rooftops.' He turned to Omari. 'We need you to get the villagers away from the houses on this side of the village. I don't want any civilian casualties.'

'Right,' nodded Omari.

'Afterwards, I suggest you get back and stay with the vehicles. The Taliban look like they outnumber us. In case this doesn't go as we hope, you'd better make sure you get away.'

Omari hesitated. 'I'm supposed to be with you,' he said.

'You're supposed to stay alive,' said Nelson firmly.

'OK,' agreed Omari. He hurried off to urge the villagers to safety.

Gaz ran down from the roof. 'ETA, seven minutes,' he announced. 'I count fourteen of them. All armed.'

'I wonder if they know we're here?' murmured Nelson in Tug's earshot.

'I don't think so,' said Tug. 'If they knew that they wouldn't be marching in the way they are; they'd be coming in on different sides and mounting a proper guerrilla attack. No, I'm sure this is just a punishment visit.'

'OK, take your positions, guys,' said Nelson. 'I'll go with Two Moons. Benny and Tug together. Mitch and Gaz.'

The soldiers headed towards the three buildings that looked out towards the desert. Mitch and Gaz ran up the steps and crawled across the baked mud of the roof to the edge and peered out.

Through his binoculars Mitch could make out the Taliban fighters' weapons. Most of them appeared to be carrying Kalashnikov AK-74s. That made sense when the fighters were on foot. It was a relatively light gun: thirteen pounds unloaded, lighter than the AK47. There were quite a few in Afghanistan. With a firing rate of 650 rounds a minute, it was a solid, trustworthy rifle.

The fourteen Taliban fighters were nearly at the

village now. They were moving very confidently, sure of their purpose. Mitch could see their eyes. Men on a holy mission, armed and very, very dangerous. To them, there was only one correct way of living: their way.

Mitch and Gaz levelled their rifles, ready to go into action, when suddenly they heard gunfire from inside the village.

14

The effect on the Taliban was immediate. The fighters ran to the nearest cover, ducking and crouching low as they ran, just as Nelson and the men of Delta Unit opened fire.

'Gaz! See what that shooting is!' Nelson's voice ordered in their earpieces.

'I'm on it!' responded Gaz. He slid across the roof to the village side and dropped down to the ground. The shots from inside the village had stopped, now there was a mix of shooting from Delta Unit and the return fire of the Taliban fighters from behind the rocks and ridges of sand.

'No sign of hostiles in the village,' came Gaz's voice. 'I reckon it was a warning to alert the Taliban.'

'Stay village side, Gaz,' ordered Nelson. 'Just in

case whoever it was decides to launch an attack from inside.'

'Got it,' confirmed Gaz.

Mitch took a break from firing and looked across at the next roof. Two Moons had the grenade launcher on his shoulder, taking aim. There was a *whoosh!* as the launcher fired, and the grenade sailed through the air, exploding right on the Taliban lines.

Fire and black smoke belched out where it struck. There were yells and return gunfire, but it was obvious Two Moons' shot had had an effect. Mitch saw some of the Taliban fighters get up from the area near where the grenade had hit and run for better cover. Mitch let off a burst of bullets and saw two of the Taliban go down as they ran.

The Taliban launched a new attack and their shooting now came from a different direction. Two Moons delivered two grenades and the gunfire fell silent.

Suddenly five figures rose up from behind the

ridges of rock and sand and began to run towards the village, firing wildly, bullets from their automatic rifles spattering the houses and ricocheting off the rocks. It was a desperate attempt at an attack. Against a lesser opponent it might have worked, but the soldiers of Delta Unit were professionals. They shot at the advancing Taliban, who fell to the ground.

The firing from the Taliban fighters had now stopped completely.

'Give it a minute,' warned Nelson. 'Just in case it's a trick.'

They waited and let the seconds tick by. Then Nelson said, 'OK. Mitch, Benny and Tug, go check the bodies. Gaz, give Two Moons a hand in getting the ordnance back to the vehicle. I'll try and find out what happened in the village.'

Mitch came down from the roof, then he, Tug and Benny moved out towards the Taliban lines. They kept a good distance between each other, alert and waiting for one of the fighters to rise and take shots at them. But nothing happened.

The Taliban fighters were all dead.

'Body count,' said Tug.

They counted. Nine dead Taliban behind the ridge. Five in the open area near the village. Fourteen bodies. All accounted for.

15

Benny, Tug and Mitch headed back to the village. They arrived in the square to find Nelson and Omari talking to Parwaz Shah. Omari was translating, while Two Moons and Gaz stood watching.

Parwaz Shah looked very unhappy indeed. He was gesturing out towards the desert, and at the surrounding houses, and there was no mistaking the urgency and plaintiveness in his voice. It was noticeable that none of the other villagers were out on the street: they had all chosen to remain indoors.

'What's he saying?' Mitch asked.

'He's unhappy we killed the Taliban,' said Omari. 'He's afraid there'll be retribution.'

'You mean he'd have preferred the Taliban to carry out their punishment?' asked Benny.

'Maybe,' said Omari.

Suddenly Tug strode towards Parwaz Shah and threw a question at him in Pushtu. Although Tug was doing his very best to keep himself under control, to the others it was obvious he was angry. Shah glared at Tug and snapped something back, then stormed off towards his house.

'Guess friendly relations have just broken down,' muttered Two Moons.

'What did you ask him?' Nelson asked Tug.

'I just asked him who fired that shot,' said Tug.

Omari shook his head. 'No,' he corrected him. 'Your manner suggested that you were accusing him of being involved.'

'Can you be sure he wasn't?' demanded Tug.

Omari shrugged. 'I don't know,' he admitted. 'But I think we've outstayed our welcome here. It's time we moved on – and fast.'

The question of who had fired the warning shot was the main topic of conversation for Mitch, Gaz and

Two Moons as they drove along. Once again they were bringing up the rear of the convoy. When they had exhausted that topic, their conversation turned to the journey and their mission ahead.

'How far you reckon we got to go before we hit Kajaki District?' Two Moons asked.

Mitch checked the satellite navigation system. 'I calculate another twenty miles,' he said.

The convoy crawled along the main road through the desert, rocky hills rising up on either side of them.

They had been travelling for just over an hour when Nelson's voice came over the radio: 'Rocks across the road ahead.'

'Rockfall?' came Tug's voice.

'Nix that,' said Nelson. 'Looks like another ambush. Everybody back!'

Mitch immediately swung the wheel, bumping the vehicle in a circle to turn it back the way they had come, but as he did so an explosion at the side of the road threw rocks and dust across the track in front of them. Another explosion went off, and more rocks rained down in a cloud of choking dust.

'Why didn't the detector pick up those IEDs?' demanded Gaz.

'Because they're not roadside IEDs,' said Mitch. 'That was a rocket-propelled grenade.' Into the radio he relayed the message to the other vehicles: 'The road's cut off this way. RPGs flying everywhere.'

'OK, group up,' said Nelson.

Once again, Mitch swung the Humvee round and headed towards Tug and Benny's car. Even as he did so, bullets were ricocheting off the armour of the vehicle and the rocks around them.

Tug had pulled his car to a halt. Nelson's vehicle joined them from the other direction.

'Triangle,' commanded Nelson. 'Circle those wagons.'

They put the three armoured cars into a protective triangle, and then spilled out into the area of shelter between them. All the time bullets thudded into the ground and pinged off the metal.

'Let me guess. The Taliban?' said Nelson.

Omari nodded. 'This is no coincidence,' he said grimly. 'This is revenge for killing those Taliban back in the village.'

'How would they know that was us? We got them all,' said Nelson.

'I guess not everyone in that village thinks the Taliban are a bad thing,' commented Tug bitterly. 'Remember, someone fired that warning shot.'

The team had already taken up firing positions behind the vehicles and were pouring tracers of bullets out into the desert. Although they couldn't see their attackers, they knew the general direction the gunfire was coming from and were set on keeping the enemy contained.

'I think I've got something,' said Two Moons, scanning the area through his binoculars. 'A position due east. They're hunkered down, using rocks and dips in the ground for cover.'

'They're over to the west and the north too,' said Mitch, also scanning the landscape.

'And the south,' added Tug. 'So I think we can truthfully say we're surrounded.'

'How many of them?' asked Nelson.

'Judging by the amount of gunfire: forty. Maybe fifty.'

'They've got at least one RPG launcher,' said Benny. 'So they could do serious damage to the vehicles, armoured or not.'

'In which case, we'll all fry,' said Tug.

'Cover me. It's time we unloaded some of our own big guns,' said Two Moons. 'Maybe level this playing field a bit, as you Brits are fond of saying. Give me a hand, Mitch?'

'You got it,' replied Mitch.

Tug, Benny and Gaz started laying down covering fire in a circular pattern, tracers of bullets tearing into rocks, ridges, scrub and the few thin, twisted trees, while Two Moons opened up the rear of one of the vehicles. He and Mitch began unloading a mortar and rounds. Swiftly, Two Moons set the mortar up on the ground, the trajectory of the shells set so they would sail over the roof of the vehicle towards the target.

'Someone give me a bearing,' said Two Moons.

Tug gave him a set of coordinates. 'There's quite a group of them there, judging by the bullets coming from that direction.'

'Then let's give 'em something to think about!' Two Moons fired off two mortar shells in rapid succession. Tug watched their flight, then focused his binoculars where they exploded.

The enemy responded with more gunfire, forcing the men to duck down and take cover. Some of the bullets found the gaps between the cars, and Tug stumbled back, clutching his chest.

'You hit?' demanded Nelson.

'No. Luckily the body armour took it,' Tug reassured him.

Nelson took Tug's position near the front and fired off a burst at the attackers.

There was the familiar *whoompf!* of an RPG being launched in the distance.

'Incoming!' yelled Two Moons.

They heard a *whoosh*, and the rocket-propelled grenade passed over the tops of the vehicles and exploded in the desert on the other side of them, not far off.

'That was close,' groaned Gaz.

'Too close!' snapped Nelson. 'If he gets his eye in, the next one will kill us.'

'We've got to take the battle to them,' said Tug. 'We use the Humvees.'

'We don't know what the conditions are off road,' Benny pointed out. 'We could get bogged down in sand.'

'But at least we'll be forcing them to spread their fire. Here, we're trapped like fish in a barrel.'

More gunfire poured into their position, bullets ricocheting around them, tearing into the ground around their feet.

'They're closing in on us,' said Nelson. 'This isn't looking good.' He turned to Omari. 'You've got a chance if you surrender.'

Omari shook his head. 'I was with you when you killed the Taliban at the village,' he said. 'We're tarred with the same brush.'

'You could tell them you were our prisoner,' said Nelson.

'Somehow I don't think they'd believe me,' said Omari.

The firing from the Taliban was getting heavier as the fighters drew nearer to their position.

'This is like Custer's Last Stand,' grunted Gaz.

'Except you got an Indian with you,' said Two Moons.

Another RPG flew over their heads, barely missing them. They responded, letting fly with tracers of bullets towards the Taliban. Suddenly Benny crashed back against one of the vehicles and slumped forwards, blood streaming down his face.

16

'Man down!' yelled Nelson.

Mitch had already slid over to Benny, who lay unconscious with a bullet wound bleeding high on his forehead. Suddenly Benny made a choking sound, and then stopped breathing.

Acting quickly, Mitch pushed Benny down on the ground so he was prone, and began to carry out CPR: pinching Benny's nostrils tight and blowing air into his lungs, then pressing down on his chest, counting silently as he did so: 1, 2, 3, 4, 5, 6, 7 . . . then blowing into Benny's mouth and lungs again. 'Come on, Benny!' he whispered urgently. 'Breathe!'

Blood from Benny's wound was running down on to the sand. Where was the bullet? Had it hit Benny in the brain?

Bullets continued to pour in from the Taliban positions. Two Moons fired off more mortars, set on keeping the enemy down. From behind the vehicles they heard the explosions as the mortars struck, but the firing just started up again even harder.

'We can't hold out much longer,' said Tug. 'We have to use the cars and make a break for it.'

As he said it, there was another *whoosh!* then one of the vehicles rocked and crumpled down on to the sand.

The men, deafened and shaken by the blast, shook their heads, recovering.

'That's one vehicle gone,' said Gaz.

Mitch continued applying CPR, blowing air into Benny and hammering away with the chest compressions, pressing harder now, willing Benny to make a sound, any sort of sound . . .

Suddenly there was a groan and a rush of air from Benny's lungs, and Mitch offered up a silent prayer of thanks.

Another burst of Taliban gunfire raked across the vehicles, making them all duck and press against the sides for cover.

'I think Tug's right, we have to take it to the enemy,' said Nelson. 'Sooner or later one of these vehicles is gonna get a direct hit and blow up, taking us with it.' To Mitch, he called, 'How's Benny doing?'

'He's alive,' said Mitch. 'Just.'

Mitch tore a strip of cloth from his costume and began to wrap it round Benny's head to staunch the flow of blood from the wound.

Suddenly they heard a huge explosion from the Taliban lines, so loud that they felt the ground shudder around them.

'What the . . .?' began Two Moons.

There was a second explosion, this one from a different position, but from the yells and screams they could tell it was a direct hit on the Taliban.

'Tank shells!' yelled Tug.

Yet another explosion tore into the Taliban

lines. Now, from their hiding place, they could see the remaining Taliban fighters running away. As they stepped out from behind the cover of the Humvees they heard the rumbling of tank tracks and the whooshing of helicopter blades. A burst of gunfire tore over their heads, making them duck, and they heard an English voice call out through a loudspeaker, 'Face down on the ground! Spread your arms!'

'OK, do as the man says,' ordered Nelson.

The men put their weapons to one side and lay down in the sand. After a while, they felt the ground beneath them shudder and tremble as the heavy tanks drew near. Then came the sound of engines and tractor wheels. Mitch began to lift his head, but the same voice from the loudspeaker rapped out, 'Stay still!' Next came the sound of boots hurrying towards them and the click of guns being prepared and aimed.

'Sarge! I think we found those drug dealers the colonel was talking about!'

17

The men of Delta Unit, along with Omari, lay face down in the sand, their hands spread out. They could see the boots of the soldiers standing guard over them. Past them they could see tanks and desert crawlers. Mitch lay next to Benny, watching him closely, making sure he was breathing even though he was unconscious.

'We've got a badly injured man here!' shouted Nelson. 'He needs urgent medical attention or he'll die!'

A voice shouted, 'Paramedics!' and two men appeared and dropped to their knees beside Benny's still body.

'How is he?' demanded Nelson.

'Shut up!' snapped one of the soldiers.

'He's alive,' said a paramedic. 'But only just.' He shouted out, 'Stretcher over here! Quickly! Get this one to Camp Bastion.' The stretcher party came running and loaded Benny on, then set off for the nearest helicopter, the paramedics hurrying alongside.

Mitch started to get up, but a rifle was jabbed into his back, forcing him back down on to the ground.

'I said stay there!' shouted the soldier.

Face down in the sand, Mitch tried to shift his body to get a better view of what was going on. Another pair of boots arrived to join the soldiers, and a new voice asked, 'Is this all of them, Sergeant?'

'Yes, sir,' barked the sergeant in a strong Geordie accent. 'We've searched the area, but there are no others. Just a few dead hostiles. One casualty being taken to Camp Bastion.'

'Good,' said the new voice. Then he addressed the men lying face down. 'Now listen. You will put your hands behind your back. My men will handcuff you. You will then stand up. Do not make any attempt to escape or resist.' Then he added, 'All right, Sergeant. Handcuff them.'

'Yes, Captain,' said the sergeant. Then, in harsher tones, he snapped at the men on the ground, 'You heard the captain. Hands behind your backs!'

The men of Delta Unit did as they were told, and the soldiers went from one to another, handcuffing them with plastic restraints.

A group of British soldiers in desert outfits stood at a safe distance, automatic rifles pointed at them. The expressions on the soldiers' faces ranged from grim stares to sneers of disgust. The captain and the sergeant stood closest to their prisoners, surveying them.

'So,' said the captain with obvious distaste. 'We've been wondering if we'd run into you. The gang of renegade soldiers who are planning to make their fortune by dealing drugs with the Taliban.'

The men of Delta Unit said nothing.

'Frankly, if it was left to me, I'd shoot the lot

of you right now,' continued the captain. 'But my colonel wants to ask you some questions about your Taliban business partners. You'll be coming with us so he can have a little chat with you.'

Although the captain's tone was cool and calm, there was no mistaking the menace in that phrase 'little chat'. The captain turned to the sergeant. 'Put them in the crawler, Sergeant.'

'Yes, sir,' the sergeant replied.

'And detail someone to bring in their vehicles.'

The captain walked away. The Geordie sergeant came closer to the men and glared at them.

'Nothing to say?' he demanded angrily. 'Well, we'll soon change that. I don't know which I hate more: a traitor or a drug dealer, but you lot seem to be both. I'm going to enjoy getting information out of you.'

The team were bundled into one of the desert crawlers and the doors were slammed shut. It was a very tight squeeze, the air hot and sticky. They heard other vehicles being started up and voices shouting commands and responses. Then the engine of their desert crawler burst into life. The vehicle began to shudder, and started to roll.

'Here we go,' murmured Mitch.

'I think we're going to be asked some interesting questions, Colonel,' said Two Moons.

'And we say nothing,' ordered Nelson.

The men nodded in agreement. All of them were thinking about Benny and wondering if he was still alive. The sight of him being rushed away to the helicopter, his face covered in blood, was an image that hung heavy over them. Gaz tried to shake it away by making light of their situation.

'This is fun,' he said. 'Sitting handcuffed in a police vehicle. It's just like being back home.'

'You and I obviously had very different backgrounds,' said Tug with a smile, joining in the attempt to lighten the atmosphere. 'I was never handcuffed during my youth.' He sighed ruefully. 'Alas, since I joined this outfit . . . '

'I know, it's happened many times, Your Lordship,' chimed in Two Moons.

'Too many,' confirmed Tug. 'I should have listened to my mother. She always warned me I'd get into bad company one day.'

From the driving area above them, the Geordie sergeant shouted out, 'Shut up down there! No more talking or I'll come down and give you all a kicking!'

Gaz grinned. 'Hear that,' he chuckled. 'Geordie hospitality! You can't beat it, pal!'

18

After hours of bone-shaking driving the desert crawler finally shuddered to a halt. The doors opened and they were ordered out. By now it was evening and darkness had descended across the desert, but here banks of floodlights blazed down on them.

'Get in line!' ordered a voice.

The men complied and took in their surroundings. From what they could see of the military buildings and equipment around them, they were at a Forward Operation Base. Since the Coalition forces had moved into Afghanistan, more and more of these FOBs had been established to push the front line into enemy territory. They were forts in the desert: a defensive front line of blocks and rocks around the base to protect against a direct attack, and what was virtually a small town of portable buildings to house the troops and support.

A lieutenant appeared from one of the nearby buildings and looked at the line of handcuffed men. There was no mistaking the look of scorn and disgust on his face as he approached them. 'Follow me!' he snapped. To the armed soldiers guarding them he ordered, 'Keep your weapons aimed at them. If they try and make a break for it, shoot them in the legs.'

With that he turned on his heel and headed back to the building.

'Come on, you!' barked the Geordie sergeant, and he prodded Gaz with the barrel of his rifle.

The handcuffed men moved forward, following the lieutenant.

Inside the building they found themselves in a command room, complete with tables, chairs, noticeboards and screens. A man got up from one of the chairs as they entered the room. Like all the soldiers he was dressed in desert fatigues, but there was no mistaking his air of authority. He waited

until Nelson and the rest of the prisoners were assembled in a line, and the armed soldiers had pulled back to a watchful distance.

'I am Colonel Taggart,' he told them. 'We received intelligence that a bunch of renegade soldiers were heading to Kajaki to negotiate a drug deal with one of the Taliban warlords, Azma Al Haq. So I asked my men to keep an eye out for any suspicious characters in the area. A gang of seven American and British soldiers. Does that description sound familiar to you, gentlemen?'

Nelson shrugged. 'We could be under cover on a special mission,' he said.

Colonel Taggart looked at Nelson coldly, and then laughed. 'Nice try,' he said. 'But, as the commander of the forces in this area, I am always informed of any special or covert missions that might be happening so that we don't interfere. Or so that we can give our assistance, if needed. I have been given no intelligence about any missions, special or otherwise, involving American and British soldiers.

However, I *have* been given intelligence about these renegade soldiers.' He smiled a cold smile. 'Guess which version of events I prefer to believe?'

Nelson gave a look of frustration, but the Colonel continued. 'Now we've got the fairy stories out of the way, let's get down to the reality. You've been caught. Frankly, your position here is . . . shall we say . . . precarious. As I'm sure you will already have gathered from my men, drug dealers and traitors aren't very popular with them. Or with me. We're fighting a war here. The last thing we need is scum like you making the situation worse. So, if you want to make things easier for yourself you can answer me one simple question: where is Al Haq's hideout?'

The handcuffed men remained silent. Taggart waited.

'Perhaps you'll tell me why you were engaged in a battle with those Taliban?' he demanded finally. 'After all, my men rescued you.'

'Let's just say it was a difference of opinion,' said Nelson.

'In other words, they don't like the idea of you muscling in on their business,' grunted Taggart. 'I'll ask you again, where is Al Haq's hideout?'

The men in the line looked straight ahead and said nothing in reply.

'Let me have a few minutes with them and I'll get the answer, Colonel,' urged the Geordie sergeant. There was no mistaking the contempt in his voice.

'I'm sure you would, Sergeant,' said Taggart, 'but let's see if we can do this the easy way first. I'd hate anything serious to happen to them and their deaths to be on your conscience.'

The sergeant shook his head as he glared at Nelson and the men. 'With respect, sir, it wouldn't be troubling to my conscience at all. They're traitors. They don't deserve to live.'

Colonel Taggart looked coolly at Nelson, and then at each of the other men in turn.

'You see how strongly my sergeant feels about what you are doing here?' he asked. 'I believe the rest of the men at this base feel exactly the same.

They are risking their lives here. We have lost many men already. Good men. The idea that criminals like you are trying to make money out of the situation makes me sick to my stomach. You are worse than criminals. You are a disgrace to the uniforms you wore. You are traitors to every man here. So, as I say, if you want to get out of this camp in one piece I would strongly recommend you tell me where Al Haq's mountain hideout is.'

Taggart's expression grew darker and he added angrily, 'In case you're not aware of the current situation, Azma Al Haq's forces have recently stepped up their attacks on our troops. Previously, they have kept to their own region, but lately they seem to have come south to join forces with the Taliban in this locality. In the last week I've lost six men to his forces, with another seventeen seriously wounded.'

At this, Mitch shot a brief glance of concern at Two Moons.

'So I ask you again, for the lives of the men here,

where is the hideout?' barked Taggart.

Delta Unit remained mute. Taggart looked at them as if he wanted to spit in disgust.

'Very well,' he said. 'Sergeant, check them for concealed weapons, then lock them up.'

'Yes, sir!' responded the sergeant.

He put down his rifle and picked up a small hand-held metal detector, and ran it over the men. In this way he found Mitch's M23 and both his knives, as well as the weapons concealed by the others.

As the weapons were dumped in a pile by the Sergeant, Taggart shook his head.

'An undercover armoury,' he commented.

'We're soldiers,' responded Nelson.

Taggart shook his head. 'Not in my book,' he said. 'You're filth.'

As the sergeant ran the metal detector down Tug's left side it beeped, just as it had with everyone else. The sergeant patted the left leg of Tug's uniform, and then frowned, surprised to find no sign of a weapon.

'There's nothing there. Just titanium and some nuts and bolts holding my leg together,' explained Tug. 'I was wounded a couple of months ago.'

'Oh really!' sneered the sergeant. He pulled a knife from his belt and slit the leg of Tug's trousers at the thigh, then ripped it open. Everyone could now see where the repairs to Tug's leg had been carried out: the scars and the marks where the stitches had been. Even the sergeant and Taggart could see they were relatively fresh.

The sergeant shot a questioning look at Taggart, who nodded uncomfortably.

'Very well,' he said. 'Right, Sergeant. Lock them up now.'

As the men were about to be taken out, Nelson stopped and turned to Taggart.

'One last thing, Colonel. Is there any news of our comrade?' he asked.

'He's at Camp Bastion,' said Taggart curtly.

'I know where he is,' retorted Nelson. 'I want to know what his condition is.'

'You're in no position to demand anything,' Taggart shot back. Then his tone softened slightly and he added, 'Latest reports say he's alive and is being operated on. I believe a bullet penetrated his skull. I don't have any more details than that.' He glared at Nelson and continued, 'With the skill of the surgeons and a bit of luck he'll be able to stand trial with the rest of you.'

Mitch and Two Moons exchanged looks of relief. Benny was still alive. That was the main thing.

As the sergeant prodded Nelson with his rifle to take the men away, Taggart stopped them.

'This is your last chance to do something decent. Tell us where Al Haq's hideout is.'

'And if we don't?'

'Then you'll be put on the next plane back to England, where you'll be arrested.'

19

They were taken to a large building at the centre of the base. In the main room were four huge cages. The soldiers unlocked the doors of two of them, took the plastic restraints off the team and pushed them inside: Nelson, Tug, and Omari into one cage; Mitch, Two Moons, and Gaz into the other. There was nowhere to sit in the cages, except what looked like a portable steel toilet in one corner of each, welded firmly to the bars.

The soldiers who had ushered them into the cages left, but Mitch could see through the half-open door that two others had been left on duty to guard them. The men of Delta Unit squatted down inside the cages, near the bars so they could talk.

'We need to get out of here before they can put

us on a plane,' said Nelson. 'If they kick us out, our mission's failed.'

'Maybe we should tell Colonel Taggart the truth?' suggested Omari.

Nelson shook his head. 'No. According to Taggart, Al Haq's men have stepped up their action recently and they've killed six of Taggart's men. That's not going to make him sympathetic to our mission. He wants to kill Al Haq, not talk to him.'

'That's one thing that puzzles me, big time,' said Mitch, frowning. He turned to Omari. 'If Al Haq is as keen to talk peace as you say he is, why is he going on the offensive in this way?'

Omari shrugged, a puzzled expression on his face. 'I don't know,' he admitted. 'Perhaps he's bluffing, trying to convince the Taliban he's serious in his support for their cause.'

'Or maybe he never really planned to go ahead with the peace talks,' suggested Tug. 'In which case we would be really stupid to carry on with this mission.'

There was an awkward silence, during which the men looked first at Omari, and then at Nelson. 'I, for one, am gonna be really mad if Benny dies because we've been suckered by this uncle of yours,' grunted Two Moons. There was no mistaking the anger in his voice as he looked at Omari.

'Hold it,' ordered Nelson. 'We don't know for sure Al Haq has changed his mind.'

'But stepping up the attacks certainly suggests it,' said Tug pointedly.

'No!' said Omari firmly. 'I am certain my uncle did not lie to me when we met. He wants peace, I am absolutely convinced of it. He told me that he was sick of his children and grandchildren dying in a war. He wants an Afghanistan where they can live without fear.'

'Well, he's sure got a funny way of showing it,' muttered Mitch.

Once again, the men of Delta Unit looked at Nelson for direction. The colonel regarded Omari thoughtfully for a while, then he asked: 'You're prepared to stake your life on your uncle's word?'

Omari nodded. 'Yes, I am,' he said.

'OK,' said Nelson. 'Then so are we. We go on with the mission.' He looked at the men of his unit. 'That right, fellas?'

The men hesitated, then nodded.

'If you say it's OK, Colonel, then I'm with you,' said Two Moons.

'Me too,' agreed Mitch.

Tug and Gaz nodded.

'Good,' said Nelson. 'The other reason I'm not going to tell Colonel Taggart the truth is because he'd then have to do one of two things,' continued Nelson, 'Give us an escort to Al Haq's hideout . . .'

'Out of the question!' said Omari firmly. 'That would ruin everything.'

'. . . or let us go. And if he did that he'd have to tell his commanders the truth. And sooner or later one of them would mention why we'd been let go, and what our mission was. And that word would be picked up by some of the locals.'

Omari nodded. 'I see what you mean,' he said.

'So, like I said at the outset, if this mission is to go ahead, we have to get out of here on our own terms, right now. Any ideas?'

Tug gestured at the cages they were being held in. 'These bars are solid steel. They're sunk into cement all the way round at the base. We don't have any equipment we can use to cut our way out, and even if we did the guys outside would hear it and be in here in a flash.'

'Yes, that's true,' agreed Nelson. 'So we have to be a bit shrewd.' He looked through the bars at Mitch, Two Moons and Gaz. 'Any of you fellas feel like dying?' he said, smiling.

The three soldiers exchanged thoughtful looks, then Two Moons laughed and said: 'I think it better be me.'

Omari gaped at Nelson. 'What do you mean?' he demanded.

'Wait and see, pal,' Gaz told Omari. 'Your job is to shout.'

Omari looked at Gaz bewildered. 'I don't understand,' he said.

'You will.' Gaz grinned. To Two Moons, he said, 'You and me, then?'

'Both of you!' said Two Moons indignantly. 'I've got too much pride to be killed by just one man.'

'Right,' agreed Mitch.

With that, he and Gaz rushed at Two Moons. Both men leapt on the big Indian and began to punch him. Two Moons fought back, blocking their punches and delivering blows of his own, and all three men collapsed in a brawling heap on the ground.

Nelson looked at Omari. 'OK,' he said. 'This is where you start shouting.'

Omari gaped at him, and at the three men fighting in the next cage, and suddenly he realised what was happening.

'Stop it!' he yelled. 'Stop it! Guards! Guards!'

The commotion brought the two soldiers on duty running in. They levelled their rifles at the three men fighting in the cage.

'Stop it now!' ordered one.

Reluctantly, Gaz and Mitch struggled to their feet and staggered back. Two Moons lay still on the ground, his mouth and eyes open, staring at nothing.

'You! Get up!' commanded the soldier angrily.

Two Moons didn't move.

Mitch stepped towards the fallen Sioux. 'Come on, Two Moons!' he said. 'Game over! Get up!'

Two Moons stayed where he had fallen, dead still.

A worried expression crossed Mitch's face. He bent down, and then knelt beside Two Moons.

'Get up!' shouted the soldier.

Mitch ignored him. He felt Two Moons' neck, then his wrist. He stood up, and now he looked shaken.

'He's dead,' he said.

'He can't be!' exploded Gaz. 'I hardly touched him!'

'It must have been his heart,' said Nelson. 'He was due to have a medical just before we came out.

I knew he was hiding something from us!'

One of the soldiers gestured impatiently at the men in the cage standing around Two Moons' still body. 'Get your hands up, all of you!' he ordered.

Mitch and Gaz obediently raised their hands.

'Get back against the side of the cage!' ordered the soldier.

The two men did as they were told. One of the soldiers kept his gun pointed firmly at the prisoners, while the other produced a key and unlocked the door of the cage where Two Moons lay.

'Put your hands on your heads and walk out in single file,' ordered the soldier with the rifle.

Mitch and Gaz shuffled out of the cage.

The soldier with the rifle now turned his attention to the other cage, the one that held Nelson, Omari and Tug.

'You lot,' he commanded brusquely, 'hands on heads and get away from the door.'

The three men complied, moving back, away

from the cage door.

'Right, get in there with them,' the soldier snapped at Mitch and Gaz.

The two prisoners hesitated.

'Do it!' barked the soldier. 'Or one of you gets a bullet in the leg! And, believe me, I hate drug dealers just as much of the rest of the lads, so don't give me the chance!'

Mitch and Gaz shuffled into the other cage to join their fellow prisoners. As soon as they were in, the soldier slammed the door shut and locked it.

'Right,' he said to the other soldier. 'Keep your eye on this lot.'

With that, he stepped into the second cage and walked warily across to where Two Moons lay. He stood over him, rifle aimed, and waited. Two Moons just lay there, mouth and eyes open in an unblinking stare.

The soldier hesitated, then he jabbed the barrel of his rifle down into Two Moons' chest. As he did so, Two Moons suddenly came to life. He grabbed the rifle barrel with both hands and shoved it back upwards so the butt caught the soldier under the chin. As the soldier began to collapse, Two Moons was up, pushing him towards the edge of the cage. When the soldier hit the bars, Tug reached through and grabbed him round the neck.

Two Moons now had the rifle in his hands and he aimed it at the other soldier, who looked back at him, stunned.

'Don't try anything,' Two Moons warned him. 'If I see your finger tighten on the trigger, I'll shoot you dead. If you call out, your friend here gets his neck broken. If you play it sensible, you and your buddy live.'

The soldier stood, shocked, his rifle aimed at Two Moons.

'I really don't want to kill you, but I will if I have to,' said Two Moons. 'All we want to do is get out of here. So throw your gun down on the ground.'

The soldier hesitated, undecided. While this was happening, Nelson reached through the bars of the cage and felt the pockets of the soldier Tug had in a stranglehold. He pulled out the key to the cage door.

'Got it,' he said.

'See?' said Two Moons. 'There's no way you can deal with all of us. Drop the gun.'

Nelson now had the door of the cage open and the rest of the men spilled out. Tug released the semi-conscious soldier and he slid down to the ground.

Nelson moved nearer to the soldier with the gun. 'Drop the gun and get in the cage,' he said, 'and no harm will come to you. Like my friend says, if we were going to kill you, you'd be dead by now. We just want to do this the easy way.'

The soldier hesitated. The prisoners had now fanned out so that even if he shot one of them, the others would be able to jump him. It was game over, and they could tell from his face that he knew it. He sighed, and dropped his rifle.

Nelson moved forwards, scooped it up and

pointed it at him. 'Join your friend inside the cage,' he said.

The soldier did as he was told.

'Tie and gag 'em,' instructed Nelson.

Mitch stepped into the cage to join Two Moons, and the pair used the soldiers' belts and socks to bind and gag them. That done, they left the cage and locked the door.

'OK,' said Nelson. 'Let's go find us some wheels.'

20

With Nelson in the lead, the men slipped out of the building that housed the makeshift jail. They immediately took cover behind stacks of boxes that were piled up nearby. Fortunately for them there was little activity inside the base: the majority of the soldiers were in the mess, and most of the patrols were at the outer perimeter, keeping watch on the surrounding desert.

'Three vehicles would be good,' said Nelson. 'Tug, Mitch and Gaz, see what you can find. We'll stay here. If too many of us start wandering around we're sure to get caught.'

Tug nodded and he, Gaz and Mitch slipped out from behind the boxes.

'Look for anything with keys in,' said Tug.

They scanned the camp. All seemed quiet.

'I think I see where they've parked everything up,' whispered Mitch. 'Over there, near the desert crawlers.'

Next to the crawlers some Snatch Land Rovers were lined up in a neat row. The men moved swiftly and silently along the wall towards them, keeping to the shadows. Suddenly, as they neared the parked vehicles, they heard the sound of boots approaching. Swiftly, the three of them dropped and rolled under the vehicles.

Mitch looked out and saw eight pairs of boots marching towards them, all hitting the ground with regular precision. It was a patrol. The approaching soldiers reached the vehicles and stopped.

'Right, squad! Standard search!' barked the patrol leader.

Mitch's heart sank. They were bound to be discovered. Eight against three, and the eight soldiers were all armed.

'Fall out, Rogers, Baker, Moran!' continued the

patrol leader.

Mitch saw three pairs of boots separate from the rest, then the other five soldiers of the patrol marched off elsewhere. At least that had cut the immediate opposition down to three; but any commotion would bring the rest of the patrol running back.

'Standard search!' repeated one of the soldiers bitterly, obviously fed up. 'What a waste of time!'

'It's got to be done, Rog,' said another. 'I mean, say the Taliban had slipped in and were here.'

'There are patrols all over the outside of the base,' said Rog. 'How they gonna get in? It's a waste of time!'

'The sooner we get it done, the sooner we can finish and get ourselves a cuppa,' said a third voice. 'I'll start with this one. You two work your way along the line.'

Mitch looked across at Tug, lying beneath the vehicle next to him, and mimed throwing a punch. Tug gave a thumbs up to show he understood.

Mitch heard the sounds of boots scuffling as the

three soldiers moved between the vehicles, checking for any movement. Mitch could tell they had done this so often before, and always found nothing, that they didn't expect anything this time. Good, he thought. So long as they're not alert. A tense soldier expecting trouble is liable to start shooting first and ask questions afterwards.

The soldier nearest to Mitch stopped and dropped to his knees. Mitch could hear his uniform rustle as he bent lower, and then a face appeared in the space between the bottom of the vehicle and the ground.

Wompf!

Mitch's fist lashed out, connecting with the soldier's chin. There was no time for the soldier to cry out: the punch knocked him out instantly. The sounds of scuffling nearby told Mitch that Gaz and Tug had dealt with their soldiers the same way.

The three men rolled out from under the vehicles. Gaz picked up a fallen rifle. 'Weapons as well!' he said, grinning happily. 'I wondered what we were going to do with just two rifles.'

'Come on,' said Tug urgently. 'Let's move!'

They searched the row of vehicles, and found that just two had keys in their ignition.

'Either someone's been careless, or they're kept like that for an emergency get away,' muttered Mitch.

'Right now, an emergency get away is exactly what we're after,' said Tug. 'OK, Mitch, go and fetch the others.'

Mitch ran off, keeping to the shadows, and returned to Nelson, Two Moons and Omari, who were still hiding behind the stacks of boxes. 'We've got just two vehicles,' he told them.

'Better than nothing,' said Nelson. 'Let's go.'

They hurried to the Land Rovers and scrambled in: Nelson, Tug and Omari in one; Mitch, Gaz and Two Moons in the other.

They started up the vehicles and then rolled them forwards, heading for the main gate of the base.

Two soldiers were standing on duty, and they

turned at the sound of their approach. One of the soldiers stepped into the gateway, his hand held up for the vehicles to stop. Gaz, who was driving the lead Land Rover, slowed down.

'What are you doing?' hissed Two Moons. 'Floor it!'

'In a moment,' said Gaz. 'When we're near enough. Right now he'd have time to get a shot in.'

Gaz slowed the vehicle down. Behind him Nelson also slowed. Then, just as they were about to stop, Gaz accelerated. The 4x4 leapt forwards, engine racing. The soldier, startled, threw himself to one side as the Land Rover tore through the gates out into the desert, with Nelson's vehicle following close behind.

Gunfire opened up from behind them and bullets bounced off the vehicles' armour. Both Gaz and Nelson slammed down on the accelerators, heading out into the desert as fast as they could.

21

They drove for half an hour, constantly checking the mirrors, expecting to be chased. But nothing appeared.

'I guess they're not following us in case it's a trap,' said Mitch.

'Makes sense,' said Two Moons. 'We renegades can be sneaky people!'

'It might be a good idea to pull over,' said Gaz. 'Meet up and see what the plan is.' He slowed down and pulled the Land Rover to a halt. The second vehicle pulled up behind them, and Nelson, Tug and Omari joined them.

'Good work,' Tug complimented Gaz. 'Nice driving.'

'I think we ought to stay here until we can see

where we're going,' Nelson proposed. 'If we see anyone coming after us we can take off, but I don't think they will. Not until daylight.'

As dawn rose the next morning, the two vehicles were already rolling. They now had black scarves tied to their aerials to identify the unit to Al Haq's forces, as Omari had arranged with his uncle.

'I wonder how Benny's doing?' murmured Gaz.

'The medics at Camp Bastion are the best you can get,' said Mitch. 'If anyone can pull him through, they can.'

'They may be able to pull him through, but what state will he be in after getting a bullet in the head?'

'Depends where they hit him,' said Mitch.

'Trouble is, there ain't many places inside the skull except the brain,' Two Moons pointed out.

At this thought, they fell silent. They all knew the implications: Benny was a soldier. Damage to the brain would put him out of action permanently.

Mitch drove on. After an hour they reached the

edge of the desert where it joined the mountains, a towering and forbidding range of peaks and rocks carved by the wind and sand into weird shapes. Breaking the silence, Two Moons voiced another concern: 'This business of Al Haq increasing his attacks on the Coalition troops,' he said. 'I don't know what you fellas think, but despite what Omari says, these attacks don't square with the idea of Al Haq wanting to talk peace.'

'No, they don't,' agreed Mitch, frowning. 'It's been worrying me, too. We just need to be extra careful, I guess. I wonder what Nelson thinks about it.'

They eased round a bend and Tug began to slow the lead vehicle. A wreck of a car had been left across the road.

Mitch slowed the second vehicle round the bend, and then pulled to a halt as he saw Omari, Nelson and Tug standing by the beaten-up vehicle blocking their way. They saw Nelson gesturing for them to get out. They joined the others on the road.

'What now?' asked Mitch.

'Either it's an ambush, or we've arrived,' muttered Nelson.

'This is where we wait,' said Omari. 'But leave the talking to me.'

They didn't have to wait long. Armed men appeared from behind the rocks, moving slowly and cautiously towards them, automatic rifles ready for action. The men wore the black turbans and scarves of the Taliban.

'No sudden moves,' ordered Nelson. 'Let Omari handle this.'

Omari stepped forward towards the Taliban fighters, holding his hands above his head to show he was unarmed. As the men of Delta Unit watched, he began to engage in conversation with the Taliban, involving plenty of arm waving and gesturing at the two Land Rovers.

Finally, Omari headed back towards the cars. 'We're expected,' he said. 'We get back in our vehicles and follow them.'

Some of the Taliban fighters had gone to the

battered vehicle. They got into it, started it up, and manoeuvred it into a position ready to roll. Then they were off.

'Looks like we're finally entering the lion's den,' commented Gaz.

22

The convoy drove about two miles along the main mountain road, then turned on to a narrow track heading deeper into the mountains. The track went up and up until they turned off again on to a twisting, bumpy, rock-strewn path with steep drops on one side.

'This is one road I wouldn't want to drive on at night,' commented Mitch.

They were now high in the mountains, the sand of the desert behind them, bare rocks surrounding them. Finally they came to a plateau, and Mitch could see large cave entrances in the rocks. He expected the lead car to pull up, but to his surprise it drove on into one of the caves. The first Land Rover followed it, and Mitch rolled their vehicle in behind.

The Taliban vehicle stopped and the fighters got out.

'This is our stop,' said Nelson's voice over the radio.

As the Delta Unit soldiers climbed out of their 4x4s, carrying their rifles, Omari hurried to them and held up his hands in a warning sign. 'No weapons!' he said.

The soldiers exchanged concerned looks. 'No weapons?' said Tug doubtfully. 'That's going to put us at a serious disadvantage.'

'You're already at a disadvantage,' Omari pointed out. 'You're heavily outnumbered. If we want to get out of here alive, we have to do as Al Haq says.'

'And you believe he'll keep his word?' asked Mitch acidly.

'Right now, we don't have any other option,' said Omari. 'And this is what we came here for.'

'Omari's right,' said Nelson. 'Believe me, I don't like this any more than you guys. But this is what we signed on for. Now we're here, let's finish it.'

Reluctantly, Mitch and the others put their guns back in the Land Rover. They were now surrounded by tribesmen, all armed.

'I guess we walk from here,' said Two Moons.

They followed Omari and the armed men further into the cave. It led into a high tunnel, carved out of the rock, with more tunnels leading off to either side.

'This is some cave,' murmured Gaz. 'You could hide an army here.'

'Al Haq has,' said Omari. 'For many years.'

'And bringing the vehicles inside the caves means nothing is ever spotted from the air,' commented Mitch. 'Neat.'

They walked for what Mitch estimated to be around half a mile, deeper into the mountain and the network of tunnels. Dim light filtered in from holes that had been dug in the ceiling up to the surface. Finally they reached an area that had been carved into a meeting space, with tables and chairs. A bearded man sat on one of the chairs, obviously waiting for them. Armed men stood guard on either side of him.

Mitch peered at the man and was surprised by how young he looked beneath the beard. Surely this couldn't be Azma Al Haq? This man looked to be in his early thirties.

The men of Delta Unit moved to one side to let Omari do the talking.

As Omari spoke, Tug whispered a brief translation to the others.

'This isn't Al Haq,' he said.

'So where is he?'

'That's what Omari's asking.'

They watched and listened as Omari and the man spoke rapidly in Pushtu.

'This isn't good,' murmured Tug.

'Why?' asked Two Moons.

'It seems the guy in the chair – his name's Arun – is one of Al Haq's sons. He just told Omari that he and his men are holding Al Haq somewhere for his own safe keeping.'

'Why?' Two Moons asked again.

'Because he has become weak. Too weak to be the leader.'

'Let me guess: because he was prepared to talk peace?' asked Nelson.

Tug nodded. 'Omari's asking if he can see Al Haq and talk to him, but Arun says there is no point. Al Haq is no longer the leader of the tribe. Arun is now the leader, along with his brother Majid.'

'So why did they let us come here?' asked Gaz.

'They want hostages,' muttered Mitch.

Tug nodded ruefully, watching as Omari made an appeal to Arun. Arun's reply was curt. There was no mistaking the look of shock and despair on Omari's face. He began talking again, gesturing desperately at the men of Delta Unit as he spoke.

'He's asking Arun to let us go,' translated Tug. 'He's telling him we came on his word of honour that we would get safe passage . . .'

Arun leapt to his feet and snapped something in angry tones at Omari.

'Let me guess, the guy's saying, "So what?"' murmured Two Moons.

'In so many words,' Tug confirmed. 'He's just told Omari that the word of an infidel has no honour here. That Omari had no right to give such a promise.'

Omari began to argue hotly, but again Arun cut him off with a few sharp words.

'So it looks as if we're stuck,' said Two Moons.

'It doesn't look good,' Tug agreed, shaking his head sadly.

Arun shouted at Omari in Pushtu, and then he turned to the men of Delta Unit, gesturing and shouting at them, too.

'He's telling Omari what he plans to do with us,' Tug translated.

'Does it include chopping our heads off on camera?' asked Gaz.

'I think he's got something else in mind,' said Tug. 'Shooting us one by one. But still on camera.'

Arun barked an order, and his armed guards

levelled their rifles at Delta Unit. One of them jabbed Omari in the ribs and gestured to him to join Nelson and the others.

'I'm sorry,' said Omari. 'It seems my uncle . . .'

'We got the picture,' Nelson told him.

Arun gave another order and the armed Taliban pushed them out of the meeting area and along the tunnel towards a door. The men were thrown roughly inside. It took a while for their eyes to adjust to the dim light, then each sank down to the ground.

Omari groaned and hung his head in despair. 'I am so sorry,' he said. His tone was bitter and despairing. 'I was certain my uncle had a strong hold on the situation. I had no idea that my cousins were planning this! When I met them with my uncle they seemed to be under his control!'

'Families, eh!' sighed Gaz.

'At least now we know why Al Haq's forces have stepped up their actions against the Coalition lately,' said Mitch.

'So what happens now?' asked Nelson.

'According to Arun, we choose,' said Tug.

All the others looked at him, puzzled. 'Choose what?' asked Gaz.

'Which one of us dies first,' explained Tug. 'Isn't that right, Mr Omari?'

23

Omari bowed his head even lower, and then nodded. 'It's his sick idea of a game,' he said. 'They plan to film you being executed, along with a demand to the Coalition.'

'And the demand is that the Coalition gets out of Afghanistan?' asked Gaz.

Omari nodded. 'Yes,' he confirmed. Then he looked up at the others, his expression defiant. 'But I will tell them to take me first, of course. I volunteer.'

'Are you nuts?' exploded Two Moons.

'It has to be me,' insisted Omari. 'I'm the one who brought you here. This is my fault.'

'That's very noble of you, but there's one problem,' pointed out Mitch. 'To them, you're not a Westerner. They don't want you, they want one of us.'

'Forget it, we're not choosing anyone,' said Nelson firmly. 'Doing that will only give this Arun guy a kick of pleasure. If they want to kill one of us, let them choose.'

'Maybe we can take them down when they come for us,' suggested Two Moons.

'We could try, but they'll be holding automatic rifles on us as they open that door,' Nelson pointed out. 'One of us makes a move and we're all dead.'

'But they want to keep at least some of you alive so they can show you off,' said Omari hopefully.

Mitch shook his head. 'All they need is to show one of us on camera being shot in the head,' he told Omari. 'They tell the world the rest of us are being held prisoner: they prop our dead bodies up against a wall and claim we're unconscious or something.'

'So what do we do?' asked Omari.

Nelson shrugged. 'We play it by ear,' he said. 'If we see an opportunity to make a break for it, we grab it. We've got nothing to lose.'

'Yeah, right,' scoffed Two Moons. 'We're about half a mile underground in a Taliban stronghold, locked in a dark room, with no weapons, and with a whole army of heavily armed Taliban warriors all over the place.'

'You got a better plan, Two Moons?' demanded Nelson.

Two Moons shook his head. 'Nope,' he said. 'I guess it sounds as good a plan as any.'

'Actually, we're not completely without weapons,' said Tug.

As the others looked at him questioningly, Tug reached down to his boot and pulled out a very small handgun.

'How did you slip that past the metal detector at the army base?' demanded Gaz.

Mitch let out a laugh as he realised. 'Because it's not metal,' he said. 'Ceramic. Right?'

Tug nodded. 'Absolutely. I thought it might come in handy.' He hefted it in his hand. 'This is a small version so it doesn't pack much of a punch. But it's easy to hide and it's certainly better than nothing.'

'What about bullets?' asked Gaz.

Tug grinned and tapped the skin on the back of his knee. A large plaster had been stuck there. The others had thought it was to cover up a bad wound that was still healing. Tug tore off the plaster and showed it to the others. There were four small bullets inside.

'So that's what set the metal detector off!' laughed Mitch. 'Tug, I've got to hand it to you! If the sergeant at the base had looked any closer at your injuries he'd have found those. You are one smooth guy!'

Two Moons and Gaz watched in admiration as Tug loaded the four bullets into the small ceramic pistol. 'That is neat!' said Two Moons. 'I'm gonna get me one of those for our next mission just as soon as we get out of here.'

'*If* we get out of here,' said Omari miserably.

'At least we've got a gun,' pointed out Gaz enthusiastically.

'You have one tiny little handgun with just four bullets,' replied Omari. 'Arun's men are armed to the teeth with some very heavy weapons.'

'Yes, but now we have the element of surprise on our side,' said Nelson. 'That's sometimes the best weapon you can have. With a bit of luck, this one small gun will get us some bigger weapons. But first, we need a plan.'

'We need Omari's uncle,' said Mitch.

'Right,' agreed Nelson. He turned to Omari and asked, 'Any idea where he might be?'

Omari shrugged. 'I don't know,' he said, sighing.

'Maybe he's dead?' suggested Gaz, looking concerned.

'No,' said Omari shaking his head. 'Arun would not do anything that stupid. Overthrowing his father and taking control is one thing. But *killing* a respected warlord. A Taliban hero . . . '

'But in Arun's eyes he's a traitor,' Tug pointed out. 'He was ready to do a deal with the enemy.'

Omari shook his head again. 'Even with that, Arun

would not kill his father,' he said firmly. 'My uncle has many loyal followers in his tribe. If Arun killed him there would be danger of a divide. He cannot afford that. The Taliban will be looking to Arun to make this tribe stronger by his actions, not weaker.'

'So if we can get out of here, get to Al Haq and spring him, maybe we can turn the tables on your cousin,' suggested Mitch. 'You know, get your uncle to rouse his followers. Attack Arun's people. Take back control.'

Omari sat, thinking about it. 'It is possible,' he said. 'But we would need to neutralise Arun and Majid. Preferably without killing them. Their deaths could lead to an inter-tribal battle, and Al Haq's power as a warlord would be greatly reduced,' he said. 'The point of this whole mission was to get Al Haq to start a peace process that will spread among other moderate Taliban. That won't happen if his power is cut in half.'

'How strong is your uncle?' asked Nelson. 'Not physically, but as a leader.'

'Very,' said Omari. 'He has led this tribe for decades.' He shook his head. 'Arun and Majid must have played some sort of trick to catch him out and imprison him.'

'Then I'm pretty sure that if we can release him to deal with Arun and Majid, he'll unite the tribe again,' said Tug.

'The thing is, if we don't even try, we're all dead for sure and so's this mission,' added Nelson firmly.

Omari hesitated, then nodded. 'You're right,' he said. 'We have to try.'

'Good,' said Nelson.

The door opened and three armed tribesmen entered, pointing their rifles at the men. One of them barked out an order in Pushtu.

'He says we are to stand against the far wall,' translated Omari. 'Except for the one we have chosen to be the first victim. He will go with them.'

'I guess that's me,' said Tug, getting to his feet. He grinned. 'After all, I have something the rest of you don't.'

157

The gun, thought Mitch. He must have a plan.

Tug said something in Pushtu to the men, confirming that he would be going with them.

The three tribesmen gestured with their rifles for the others to move away from the door, then stepped back to let Tug walk. One of the men kept his rifle pointed at Tug, while the other two trained theirs on the rest of the prisoners.

Tug headed for the door, his head bowed in surrender. He limped as he walked, wincing with each step. The Taliban showed no sympathy. Instead, one of them barked at him to speed up. Tug nodded wearily.

He's acting, thought Mitch. Lulling them into thinking he doesn't pose a threat.

As Tug reached the door he suddenly swung round, the ceramic pistol appearing in his hand as if by magic. There was a small *Phut!* and the man by the door staggered back, the rifle spinning away from his hand as the bullet tore into his arm. In one fluid movement Tug continued swinging his gun arm and a second bullet took another of the tribesmen through his shoulder.

Mitch was already moving and he kicked out at the third tribesman's rifle, knocking it from his grip. Two Moons came from the other side and hit the tribesman, sending him spinning across the room to crash against the rock wall.

Gaz snatched the rifle from the floor, while Mitch and Two Moons hauled the dazed tribesman to his feet.

Nelson and Tug gathered up the rifles from the two wounded Taliban.

'I thought they might be more valuable to us alive,' explained Tug, pointing at the two men, who were clutching their bleeding arms.

'Indeed,' said Omari, nodding. 'This is, after all, a peace mission.'

'Tell that to Arun,' grunted Mitch sarcastically.

'We will,' said Nelson, hefting the rifle.

24

They tied up the two wounded tribesmen with some of their own clothing. Then Omari fired questions at the third man. At first the tribesman just glared back, but Omari raised his voice, hammering home the fact that he was Al Haq's nephew and that to defy him would be a serious mistake. The anger in Omari's voice was clear for everyone to hear, and the tribesman buckled. Soon they knew where Al Haq was being held.

'OK,' said Nelson. 'Tie him up with the other two. And make sure they're well and truly gagged.'

While Two Moons and Gaz set to work securing the tribesmen, Nelson addressed the unit.

'OK, let's get a plan together! Two teams. Each one will need a Pushtu speaker. So, Omari, you go with Mitch and find your uncle. Me, Tug, Gaz and Two Moons will deal with Arun and Majid.'

Gaz handed Mitch the rifle he was holding. 'Here you are, pal,' he grinned. 'Your need is greater than mine. I'm pretty sure I'll be getting my hands on one of my own pretty soon.'

To give them a better chance of getting to Al Haq, Mitch and Omari took the clothes from the captured Taliban and put them on over their own. It might buy them a few seconds when confronting the men guarding Al Haq. In situations like this, even a moment could make the difference between life and death. When they were ready, the rest of Delta Unit slipped off one way through the tunnels to confront Arun and Majid, while Mitch and Omari headed in the other direction in search of Al Haq.

'According to the man I questioned, my uncle is being kept in a cell on the next level down,' Omari told Mitch. He pointed to a hole in the rock wall and Mitch saw that a stairway had been cut in the rocks.

'How many levels are there here?' he asked.

Omari shrugged. 'It's difficult to tell. These tunnels are not new. They were carved out by the tribes many years ago as a defence against attackers and invaders. Don't forget, the British were here before, over a hundred years ago, during the reign of your Queen Victoria. They tried to subdue the Afghan people, and failed. Then the Russians tried for ten long years during the 1980s, and they failed. And now the Coalition.' He looked around at the tunnels and sighed. 'My people have had a long time to build and develop these tunnels as protection. Every time there is a new invader, the tunnels are extended.'

'Let's hope we don't get lost in them,' said Mitch.

They crept carefully down the rock stairs to the level below. Mitch stayed alert and kept his finger on the trigger of the rifle just in case. As they stepped out from the stairs two armed men came hurrying towards them, and Mitch nearly swung the gun up, but Omari gently pushed the barrel back down. When the two men had passed, Omari whispered, 'There is a whole army down here. If you start firing at the first person you see with a gun, we won't get far. Most of them are just going about their business. Keep your head down and covered and we should be OK.'

'Which way to the cell?' asked Mitch.

Omari gestured along the tunnel. 'If our man was telling us the truth, about 150 feet from here we will come to a T-junction. My uncle is in a cell just round to the right, about another sixty-five feet. There are armed guards outside the door. Arun is taking no chances on Al Haq's supporters freeing him.'

'OK.' Mitch nodded. 'Let's get there and see how many guards we have to deal with.'

They hurried along until they came to the T-junction. Mitch peered round the corner; then he ducked back to join Omari. 'Two guards,' he said. 'The problem we have is that the sound of gunfire is going to bring more people running. If possible we have to deal with them silently. You up to taking one of them out?'

Omari frowned, concerned. 'I don't know,' he said. 'I'm not a man of action like you. I was never any good at fighting, even in the playground at school.'

Mitch nodded thoughtfully. 'OK,' he said. He offered the rifle to Omari. 'If we're going to do this silently, you take this.'

Omari looked at the rifle, shocked. 'You expect me to use this?' he asked, bewildered.

'No,' said Mitch. 'But one of us has got to be carrying a gun or they'll get suspicious, and I'd prefer to have both my hands free. All you have to do is the distraction bit.'

Omari looked puzzled.

'We'll walk up to them, quite casually, like we're supposed to be there,' said Mitch. 'You start talking to them and get one of them to look away from the other. Maybe drop something. Or point down the tunnel. Anything to get his attention away from me.'

'And what will you do?'

'Play it by ear. Right, let's go. You first in case they start talking.'

The two men stepped into the tunnel and walked towards the cell where Al Haq was being kept prisoner. Omari went first, holding the rifle. He began muttering in Pushtu to Mitch, as if they were having a conversation. Mitch entered into the act and nodded and shrugged, but at the same time he made sure he kept his head down so that his face was partly hidden by the scarf and the turban he wore.

The two armed men outside the cell door didn't appear particularly perturbed by the arrival of Omari and Mitch. One of them greeted them cheerfully as they drew near. I guess he's glad of some new company to ease the boredom, thought Mitch.

Omari stepped forward to the nearest guard, smiling and chattering in Pushtu, while Mitch moved past to the second one. Then Omari stopped and bent down, as if he'd spotted something on the floor by the door, exactly as Mitch had asked him to do. Both guards, puzzled and curious, also bent to look.

Mitch acted: he brought the edge of his hand down hard on the back of the neck of the guard nearest to him; and then swung that same hand up fast and hard into the other man's throat, as he turned round in surprise. The first guard collapsed as soon as Mitch hit him, but the second staggered back, making strangled noises. Despite his pain, he swung his rifle up. Mitch knocked the rifle barrel down with one hand, while he smashed his fist into the man's jaw.

The second guard collapsed.

'Right,' said Mitch. 'Let's see how easily this door opens.' He tried the handle, but the door was locked. 'One of these guys must have the key,' he said. 'If they have to get Al Haq out in an emergency they can't afford to hang around waiting for someone to turn up to unlock the door.'

Swiftly, Mitch began searching the bodies of the two unconscious men. Omari joined him and, digging around in their pockets, found an old iron key.

'I guess this is it,' he said.

'Let's hope so,' said Mitch.

Omari passed the gun back to Mitch and tried the key in the lock. They heard the mechanism click and the door opened.

'Right,' said Mitch. 'You go in and talk to your uncle. Tell him the situation. I'd better stay here just in case anyone walks past. We don't want them spotting that there's no one on guard here and reporting it.'

'What are we going to do about them?' asked Omari, pointing to the two unconscious tribesmen.

'We'll dump them inside the cell.'

Omari nodded and pushed the door. Mitch grabbed one of the unconscious guards and moved swiftly backwards into the cell, dragging the man with him. He had barely crossed the threshold when he felt a blow on the back of his neck, and he crashed to the rock floor, his head swimming.

25

Through his pain Mitch heard a warning shout in Pushtu from Omari, followed by another voice responding.

Mitch struggled to sit up. Omari was talking urgently to the man in the cell. This man was older but very large, tall and muscular, with a long beard and matted clothes. His face was bruised and bore the marks of recent beatings. There was no doubt that this was Azma Al Haq. As Mitch shook his head to try to clear the fog from his brain, he saw Al Haq and Omari slip out of the cell, and then reappear a second later dragging the body of the other guard.

'This is my uncle, Azma Al Haq,' Omari said.

'I guessed that,' muttered Mitch. He rubbed the

back of his neck. 'He packs a hell of a punch.'

'Usually the guards point their rifles and make him stand against the far wall before they enter the cell,' explained Omari. 'When he saw you come in the way you did, he thought it was an opportunity to escape. He is sorry if he hurt you.'

'Apology accepted,' grunted Mitch. He pushed himself to his feet and Al Haq came over to Mitch and bowed his head, placing his hand on his heart at the same time in greeting. Mitch did the same, even though bowing his head made his neck hurt even more. Then Al Haq picked up the rifles the guards had dropped. He slung one over his shoulder and hefted the other in his arms, ready for action.

'Does he have a plan?' asked Mitch.

'He says he is going to kill Arun.'

Mitch frowned. 'I thought you said that wasn't a good thing,' he pointed out.

'I did. But Arun seems to have been doing some very bad things to those of my uncle's people who wouldn't support him.'

Suddenly they heard the muffled sound of automatic gunfire.

'Sounds like the others have met resistance,' said Mitch.

Al Haq shouted something in Pushtu, and rushed out of the cell door, cocking the rifle as he did so.

'Does he know he's not supposed to be shooting at our guys?' asked Mitch, concerned.

'I hope so,' replied Omari.

'Then let's go with him and make sure he doesn't,' said Mitch firmly.

On the level above, Nelson, Tug, Two Moons and Gaz were trapped. They had managed to ambush two tribesmen and take their guns, so now each man was armed, but on their way to the meeting room where they had first seen Arun, they'd been spotted.

'We should've taken the clothes off those guys and put them on,' Two Moons said.

'Hindsight is a wonderful thing, Two Moons,' said Nelson sarcastically as he poured lead at the armed men who had them cornered.

The gunfire had drawn even more Taliban fighters to the scene. The four men of Delta Unit were bottled up, the attack coming from both sides of the tunnel, and more Taliban arriving.

Gaz had kept up a steady stream of fire, keeping the enemy at bay, but suddenly his rifle stopped chattering. 'I'm out of ammo!' he shouted to the others.

Tug shook his head. 'I'm nearly out as well,' he called back.

Gaz could only watch helplessly as Nelson, Two Moons and Tug continued firing. Then Tug's rifle stopped.

'Guess it's just you and me, Colonel,' said Two Moons.

'OK, let's save ammo,' said Nelson. 'You aim left, Two Moons, I'll aim right.' He peered cautiously round. More Taliban had come out of cover now, and were edging along the tunnel towards them from both directions.

'Go!' Nelson and Two Moons levelled their rifles and began firing, causing the Taliban fighters at the front to crumple to the ground. The men behind them stumbled. Some managed to turn and run; others fell on to the bodies of their comrades in the hail of bullets.

And then Two Moons' rifle stopped.

Two Moons turned to Nelson with an expression of weary resignation. 'Sorry, Colonel,' he said. 'I'm out as well.'

'Then I'll make sure every shot counts,' said Nelson. He fired again, and another Taliban fighter crashed to the ground.

26

'How much ammo do you think you've got left?' asked Tug.

The hammer of Nelson's rifle struck a hollow sound as he pulled the trigger, and the empty click made them all feel sick to their stomachs.

'Guess that was the end,' said Nelson. 'OK, boys, from here on it's hand to hand combat.'

'That would work if they came close enough,' said Gaz. 'But they'll just keep shooting us from a distance.'

They heard another burst of gunfire from the Taliban lines, but to their surprise none of the bullets came near them. Then came angry shouting in Pushtu and more gunfire from further down the tunnel.

'What's going on?' demanded Nelson.

'It seems Al Haq has arrived,' Tug responded, his eyes widening.

The shouting continued and then the men heard Mitch's voice calling, 'Guys! Come out! It's clear!'

'You sure of that?' called back Two Moons.

'Al Haq has given his word!' Omari called to them.

'OK,' said Nelson. 'Let's do as the man says.'

They stepped out, holding their empty rifles. The Taliban were still armed, their rifles pointing threateningly at the men of Delta Unit, but a booming voice from the back of the crowd issued an order, and the men lowered their rifles. Then Omari and Mitch appeared, flanking Al Haq. There was no mistaking his power. He pushed his way roughly through the Taliban fighters, shouting at them as he did so.

'If this is Al Haq, he's one angry dude,' muttered Two Moons.

Omari and Mitch joined them. 'My uncle, Azma

Al Haq,' said Omari.

'Just in the nick of time,' said Tug.

Gaz frowned. 'How come one man gets all these guys to stop firing?' he asked, puzzled.

'Because he is Azma Al Haq, the warlord, and he is free once more to rule these men,' said Omari. 'He has just told them if they resist him they will die.'

Al Haq was now addressing his men in fierce tones, stabbing his fingers in the direction of the tunnel. Mitch picked up the words 'Arun' and 'Majid', spat out like distasteful swear words. He didn't need Tug or Omari to translate for him to know that Al Haq was giving orders to take back the headquarters from his rebellious sons.

'If we're going to help, we need ammo,' Nelson told Omari.

Omari said something to Al Haq, who nodded and pointed at the armed men nearest him. These men obediently took their ammunition belts off and passed them to the Delta Unit soldiers.

'OK,' Nelson nodded to Omari. 'I see what you mean about your uncle. If anyone can persuade your people to talk, it's him.'

Al Haq shouted a command and then rushed down the tunnel. The other men yelled equally loudly, and hurried after him, brandishing their rifles.

'Guess that's our signal as well,' muttered Nelson.

The soldiers ran behind, reloading their rifles as they did so. Suddenly they heard firing ahead, and the crowd of men stopped and scattered to both sides of the tunnel. They all dived for what little cover there was. 'What's going on?' Nelson asked Omari.

'The men round that corner are Arun's hardline supporters,' said Omari. 'They only follow Arun.'

'Is there any other way to get to them?' asked Mitch.

Omari spoke to Al Haq, who called one of his men over. He spoke rapidly and the man nodded, and then gestured towards the soldiers.

'He's saying he will lead you to another tunnel,' translated Omari.

'Yes, I got that,' nodded Tug. To Nelson, he said, 'I suggest I go with him, Colonel.'

'Right,' nodded Nelson. 'Take Mitch, Gaz and Two Moons with you. I'll stay here with Omari and Al Haq.' He gave a wry smile. 'Protecting them is our mission, after all.'

The four soldiers set off at a run, following the tribesman down the tunnel away from the action, until they came to an abrupt halt. The tribesman gestured towards a narrow slit in one of the walls, and then slid through the opening.

'Think we can squeeze through there?' asked Two Moons, looking at the gap suspiciously.

'No problem,' said Gaz. He pushed his way through the opening. Tug was next, then Mitch, then Two Moons. They were in a very narrow, low tunnel, not much wider than a sewer pipe. Following the tribesman, they crawled along, aware of the sounds of gunfire through the rock.

'We're getting near,' said Tug.

Finally the tunnel ended, and they spilled out into a larger space. The sound of shooting now came from their right, round a bend in the rocky walls.

'Guess we're on the other side of Arun's men,' said Tug. 'Let's go get 'em.'

They crept cautiously towards the corner, rifles ready, fingers on triggers. Tug peered round and then leapt out into the tunnel, automatic rifle blazing. Mitch, Gaz and Two Moons followed, pouring hot lead at Arun's men.

Gunfire came back from the other end of the tunnel and the four Delta Unit soldiers had to scramble back to avoid being hit.

Using the bend as cover, the soldiers and the tribesman kept up a steady stream of fire, while Nelson and Al Haq's supporters continued their assault from the other side. Finally the firing from Arun's men stopped and a frantic cry of appeal was heard.

'Yes! They're surrendering!' cried Tug.

'What will happen to them?' asked Gaz.

'I'm guessing Al Haq will be merciful,' said Tug. 'It's Arun and Majid he's really after.'

The soldiers moved forwards cautiously, rifles levelled, aware that it could be a trick. But Arun's men were standing with their hands in the air, their rifles on the ground.

Al Haq, Nelson and Omari were coming from the other direction, the men behind them shouting in triumph. Al Haq approached one of Arun's men and spoke to him in Pushtu. As the man replied, Al Haq let out a roar of rage.

'Arun and Majid have gone,' said Tug. 'They ran off after the shooting started. They must have guessed how this would end up.'

Suddenly Mitch heard a rumbling sound up the tunnel, near to the entrance. 'An engine!' he said urgently. 'Someone's getting away!'

'Arun and Majid!' yelled Two Moons.

Mitch was already running up the tunnel and Two Moons, Gaz and Tug followed close behind him.

Al Haq had obviously realised what was going on because he began to run after the men, but Nelson grabbed him and pulled him back.

'Tell him we need him to stay safe!' he shouted at Omari, and Omari translated. Al Haq hesitated, then nodded and turned back to Nelson and clapped him on the shoulder.

'OK, guys!' Nelson yelled after the others. 'Finish this!'

27

Mitch broke out of the entrance to the caves and into the daylight just in time to see the two Land Rovers racing off. He looked around and saw the battered vehicle that had led them to the tunnels. He jumped in. The key was still in the ignition. He fired up the vehicle, just as the doors opened and Two Moons, Gaz and Tug scrambled into it.

'Go!' yelled Two Moons.

Mitch slammed the car into first and it leapt forwards, skidding. Mitch fought to steer it back into a straight line. Then the car was racing along, bouncing and crunching over the rocky, unmade road. He floored the accelerator, and they were soon gaining on the nearest Land Rover.

Two Moons pushed himself out through the open

window of the passenger door, hanging on to the roof with one hand, and pointing his rifle at the Land Rover with the other. A hail of bullets smashed into the 4x4, taking out the wing mirrors. Two Moons kept firing and the vehicle suddenly veered off the road and ploughed into a rock, sending up clouds of dust and smoke.

'Next one!' yelled Two Moons.

Mitch kept his foot down hard on the accelerator, pushing the battered car as fast as it would go. Two Moons began firing again but the driver of the second Land Rover knew what he was doing. The vehicle suddenly swerved to the left and a rifle barrel appeared from one of the side windows, letting off a burst. Two Moons gave a yell of pain and fell backwards, out through the window. Tug and Gaz turned and saw Two Moons roll on the dusty ground and then lie still. Gaz pushed his rifle out through the open rear window on his side, then followed it with his body, taking over from Two Moons. Tug did the same on the other side. With the car bouncing over the rocks, their aim was erratic; some of their bullets struck the Land Rover, some missed by miles.

Again, a rifle appeared at the window of the 4x4 and began firing at them; this time Gaz gave a cry and slid back down into the back seat, blood staining his shirt at the shoulder.

Tug fired again and his tracer of bullets tore into the rear wheels of the Land Rover, shredding the rubber. The vehicle lurched as the tyres burst, then it slid off the road and hit a rock. The two soldiers watched it bounce and then flip over, crashing on to its roof. Mitch screeched to a halt and he and Tug leapt out and brought their guns to bear on the overturned vehicle, bullets peppering the 4x4, shattering glass and tearing metal off the body.

One of the doors sprang open and a man crawled out, his clothes covered in blood. He called out something and held up an arm. 'It's Arun!' shouted Tug. 'He's surrendering!'

Mitch stopped firing, and Arun pulled himself to

his knees. Tug shouted something at him in Pushtu and Arun brought up one arm and put his hand on his head. His other dangled uselessly by his side. It was obviously broken. Gaz kicked open the door of the vehicle and stumbled out, his rifle cradled in his one good arm. Blood was still seeping through his uniform where he had been hit high in the shoulder.

'I'm going to see how Two Moons is,' said Mitch, and he broke into a sprint back the way they had come. As he neared the other wrecked Land Rover he saw that Two Moons was still lying on the ground in the same position.

Please don't let him be dead, Mitch prayed as he ran. Not Two Moons.

That's our trouble, Mitch thought. We think we're invincible. We go in against everything the enemy throws at us and think, it won't be me who dies, it'll be someone else. And then one day a stray bullet ends it. And the friend who was closer than a brother suddenly isn't there any more. Wiped out.

The big Sioux Indian was lying prone and still,

arms flung out, his fallen weapon near him. His face was a mess of blood. 'Wake up, you bastard!' shouted Mitch desperately. 'Wake up!'

Time seemed to stand still as Mitch fell to his knees next to his friend. Tears blurred his vision and he bit at his lip to stop them.

Mitch reached out and put his fingers to Two Moon's neck, checking for a pulse. As he did so he noticed Two Moons' leg move. He's alive! Mitch thought. Thank God!

The Sioux groaned, and then his eyes opened and he looked at Mitch, dazed.

'What happened?' he asked.

'You fell out of the car,' said Mitch. 'We thought you were a gonner. You OK?'

Two Moons felt his body: legs, arms, neck. Then examined himself for wounds.

'There's blood on your face,' Mitch told him. 'Guess a bullet must have creased your skull.'

'It's lucky I've got a hard head,' muttered Two Moons.

With Mitch's help he staggered to his feet and looked at the wrecked Land Rover nearby. 'Anyone alive in there?' he asked.

Mitch levelled his rifle at the vehicle and approached it cautiously. There were two men in the front seat, both leaning forwards with their heads on the dashboard. The doors had sprung open with the impact. He prodded the one behind the steering wheel with the barrel of his rifle. The man didn't respond. Carefully, in case it was a trick, Mitch reached in and felt for a pulse. Nothing. 'This one's dead,' he said.

Suddenly the man in the passenger seat let out a groan and stirred. 'The other one is still with us,' added Mitch. 'But he's not in any state to fight back now.'

He stepped back, keeping his rifle aimed. 'Guess we pulled it off,' he said.

28

Arun and Majid had both survived the crashes, and were now in separate cells in the lower levels of Al Haq's mountain hideout. A doctor had treated their injuries.

'What will happen to them?' Mitch asked Omari.

'That is not our concern,' said Omari with a shrug. 'That's Al Haq's problem. I imagine he will keep them alive, but under very close watch. My uncle is not a man to be fooled twice.'

The men of Delta Unit had their injuries tended to and were taken to rooms inside the hideout to rest. But rest was the last thing on their minds. Once order had been restored and a kind of calm had come to the mountain hideout, they sought out Omari in the room where he was preparing for his talks with Al Haq.

'We want to know how Benny is,' Nelson told him.

Omari looked at the five soldiers with an apologetic smile. 'I'm afraid I don't know,' he said. 'We won't find out until we get back to Kandahar.'

'That's unacceptable,' said Tug.

'Your uncle has all sorts of telecommunications, right,' said Gaz. 'We may be in the mountains in an ancient hideout, but the Taliban are hot on mobile and satellite phones. That's how they communicate the Coalition positions.'

'True.' Omari nodded.

'So what we'd like you to do is get on those phones to your UN contacts and find out how Benny is,' said Nelson.

Omari hesitated and for a moment the men thought he was going to argue. But instead he nodded and said, 'Leave it to me. I'll see what I can do.'

*

It was six hours later, after the first round of talks with Al Haq, that Omari sought out Nelson and the others.

'I'm sorry it's taken me so long to get the information you want,' he apologised. 'But the good news is the surgery was successful and your friend is making a good recovery. He's still in a bad way, but there should be no permanent damage.'

The men looked at one another in relief. 'Great news!' breathed Two Moons.

'So what happens to him?' asked Mitch. 'Is he still going to get charged with drug dealing?'

'I'm still working on that,' said Omari.

'Maybe if I can talk to your contact myself I can get it sorted out?' suggested Nelson.

Omari shook his head apologetically. 'I'm sorry,' he said. 'Our talks are still at an early stage, and my uncle is wary of allowing you to have direct communications with the outside.'

'But we fought alongside him!' protested Two Moons.

'We rescued him!' added Mitch.

'I know,' agreed Omari. 'But my uncle has stayed alive by being careful and trusting no one except his own immediate family.' He smiled. 'After what happened with Arun and Majid, I think even family will now be viewed with suspicion. And that includes me.'

Nelson sighed. 'OK. But the sooner we can get more info about Benny, the better.'

'I understand,' said Omari. 'And I'll do what I can.'

The peace talks between Omari and Al Haq went on for days. The men of Delta Unit waited, worrying endlessly about Benny. How was he doing? Had he been arrested while he was in hospital?

Finally, after four days, Omari came out from the latest round of talks with a smile on his face. 'My uncle and I have an agreement,' he told the soldiers.

'What are the terms?' asked Mitch.

Omari shot a concerned glance at Nelson, who grinned. 'Need to know only, Mitch. That's for the politicians, not us. But we've done what we came to do. Mission accomplished!'

'Right now, I need to know how we're gonna get out of here,' muttered Two Moons. 'We haven't got those Land Rovers any more and I don't fancy driving all the way back to Kandahar in the wrecks they've got here.'

'You won't have to,' Omari said. 'Part of the deal is that my uncle now talks to a UN diplomat at a friendly embassy in Kabul. A helicopter will come and collect him tomorrow. I understand they will give us a lift.'

'Travelling in style,' said Gaz, impressed. 'Sounds good to me!'

'And what about Benny?' asked Mitch.

Omari gave them a happy smile.

'The latest news I have is that he is recovering very swiftly indeed.'

'But what about the charges?' demanded Nelson.

'I can't see that Colonel Taggart wanting to let him walk free.'

'And you won't want our cover story blown,' added Tug. 'If I read it right, this first meeting in Kabul is just the start. You and your boss won't want it messed up now.'

'Your colleague is an American citizen,' said Omari. 'Let's just say, there have been some diplomatic strings pulled. Lieutenant Jaurez has already been transferred to an American military hospital in Kabul.' His smile broadened and he pulled a satellite phone from his pocket, tapped a number, and held it out to the men. 'I had him on hold,' he told them. 'I thought you'd prefer to hear from Lieutenant Juarez himself.'

Nelson snatched the phone from Omari and the men gathered round him, looking at the picture of Benny that appeared on the screen. He was sitting up in a hospital bed, with bandages around his head. 'Hi guys!' he said, smiling.

Gaz let out a huge cheer of delight and relief,

echoed by Mitch and Two Moons. 'Hey, go easy, guys!' protested Benny. 'I'm recovering from a head wound, remember.'

'How do you feel?' asked Nelson.

Benny grinned. 'For someone who took a bullet to the head – pretty good. The medicos have been brilliant. They say I'm going to be fine. By the time you get to Kabul I'll be up and running.'

'Walking might be more advisable at this stage,' said Tug with a grin.

'You got it,' said Benny. 'See you guys soon.' The screen flickered, and then went blank.

Nelson gave Omari a grateful smile. 'Thanks,' he said. 'And say thanks to your uncle. Linking up like that really was a sign of trust.'

'Let's hope it's just the first of many,' said Omari.

'Amen to that,' agreed Nelson. He turned to Tug, Two Moons, Gaz and Mitch. 'So, are you guys ready to head out?'

'And on to the next mission,' agreed Mitch.

'Give us a break, Mitch!' said Gaz, chuckling. 'I've still got bullet holes from this one.'

'Yeah, but that's what we do, ain't it?' Two Moons smiled. 'Put ourselves in the firing line.'

'Damn right!' said Mitch.

DISPATCHED
N.S.C.

JUN 29   3 02 PM '61

I. G.

978-1-4052-4780-1

NAME: Paul Mitchell

KNOWN AS: Mitch

USUKCSF UNIT: Delta

RANK: Trooper

PLACE OF BIRTH: London, England, UK

HEIGHT: 5' 11"

LANGUAGES: English, French, Dutch,

various West African languages (Yoruba, Ibo etc.)

PREFFERED WEAPON: Heckler & Koch Mark 23 pistol

SPECIALISM: extreme terrain

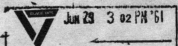

CONFIDENTIAL
(Classified)

'DISPATCHED
N.S.C.

Jun 29   3 02 PM '61

I. G.

978-1-4052-4780-1

CONFIDENTIAL

NAME: Charles Nelson

KNOWN AS: Colonel

USUKCSF UNIT: Delta

RANK: Colonel

PLACE OF BIRTH: Boston, Massachussetts, USA

HEIGHT: 6' 0"

LANGUAGES: English, Chinese, Russian, Korean

PREFFERED WEAPON: Smith & Wesson .38 Bodyguard pistol

SPECIALISM: leadership, diplomacy

978-1-4052-4780-1

NAME: Tony Two Moons

KNOWN AS: Two Moons

USUKCSF UNIT: Delta

RANK: Sergeant

PLACE OF BIRTH: Arizona, USA

HEIGHT: 5' 11"

LANGUAGES: English, Inuit, Spanish, Japanese

PREFFERED WEAPON: Ingram Model 10 sub-machine gun

SPECIALISM: ordnance, explosives

MILITARY INTELLIGEN

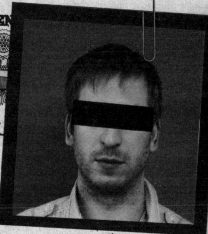

NAME: Robert Tait

KNOWN AS: Tug

USUKCSF UNIT: Delta

RANK: Captain

PLACE OF BIRTH: Oxford, England, UK

HEIGHT: 5' 7"

LANGUAGES: English, Pushtu, Farsi, Hindi, Turkish

PREFFERED WEAPON: Walther P99 pistol

SPECIALISM: leadership, diplomacy

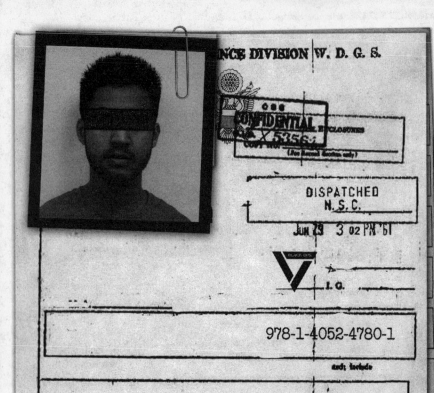

978-1-4052-4780-1

NAME: Bernardo Jaurez

KNOWN AS: Benny

USUKCSF UNIT: Delta

RANK: Lieutenant

PLACE OF BIRTH: Houston, Texas, USA.

HEIGHT: 5' 7"

LANGUAGES: English, Spanish, Polish, Greek

PREFFERED WEAPON: Ruger 0.38 Service-Six pistol.

SPECIALISM: tactics

NAME: Danny Graham

KNOWN AS: Gaz

USUKCSF UNIT: Delta

RANK: Trooper

PLACE OF BIRTH: Newcastle, England, UK

HEIGHT: 5' 6"

LANGUAGES: English, German, Italian, Norwegian

PREFFERED WEAPON: Beretta 93R pistol

SPECIALISM: recon, stealth, surveillance

EGMONT PRESS: ETHICAL PUBLISHING

Egmont Press is about turning writers into successful authors and children into passionate readers – producing books that enrich and entertain. As a responsible children's publisher, we go even further, considering the world in which our consumers are growing up.

Safety First
Naturally, all of our books meet legal safety requirements. But we go further than this; every book with play value is tested to the highest standards – if it fails, it's back to the drawing-board.

Made Fairly
We are working to ensure that the workers involved in our supply chain – the people that make our books – are treated with fairness and respect.

Responsible Forestry
We are committed to ensuring all our papers come from environmentally and socially responsible forest sources.

**For more information, please visit our website at
www.egmont.co.uk/ethical**

Mixed Sources
Product group from well-managed forests and other controlled sources
www.fsc.org   Cert no. TT-COC-002332
© 1996 Forest Stewardship Council

FSC

Egmont is passionate about helping to preserve the world's remaining ancient forests. We only use paper from legal and sustainable forest sources, so we know where every single tree comes from that goes into every paper that makes up every book.

This book is made from paper certified by the Forestry Stewardship Council (FSC), an organisation dedicated to promoting responsible management of forest resources. For more information on the FSC, please visit **www.fsc.org**. To learn more about Egmont's sustainable paper policy, please visit **www.egmont.co.uk/ethical**.